THE YEAR WHEN STARDUST FELL

Originally published in 1958

By Raymond F. Jones

And the Special Bonus Story
AND NOW A MESSAGE . . .
By Greg Fowlkes

THE YEAR WHEN STARDUST FELL

© 2010 Resurrected Press
www.ResurrectedPress.com

Published by Intrepid Ink, LLC

Intrepid Ink, LLC provides full publishing services to authors of fiction and non-fiction books, eBooks and websites. From editing to formatting, to publishing, to marketing, Intrepid Ink gets your creative works into the hands of the people who want to read them.
Find out more at www.IntrepidInk.com.

ISBN 13: 978-1-935774-40-2

Printed in the United States of America

FOREWORD

The Year When Stardust Fell was written at the peak of the cold war. Backyard fallout shelters were all the rage. The great powers were in a race to build ever more destructive bombs. Science was seen as a two edged sword. On one hand it brought marvels like television. On the other it brought the threat of total destruction. To many people, the collapse of civilization seemed just around the corner. This is the environment in which Raymond F. Jones wrote the novel.

The Year When Stardust Fell wasn't the first book to examine the collapse of civilization, and it certainly wasn't the last. "The last man alive" was a theme common in much of the science fiction of the time and had even crossed over into the more mainstream media. Indeed, visions of post-apocalyptic worlds have continue to appear in books and movies even now, sixty some years since the first atomic bomb exploded.

What sets *The Year When Stardust Fell* apart from these is that Jones gives us a detailed look at the process of the collapse, and how ordinary people try to cope with the failure of all the features of the life that they have come to count on. This is middle America at its best and its worst. Greed and cowardice is set against leadership and heroism.

It doesn't matter much that the scenario described by Jones is not very likely. He says as much in his preface. What he wanted to examine, and have the reader ponder, was how people would deal with a collapse. This is still a relevant question. It is true that nuclear war seems less likely today that it did in the 50's, at least between the major powers. But one can hardly pick up a paper without reading about environmental catastrophe from one cause or another, whether it is global warming, genetic engineering or whatever. And let's not forget old-fashioned natural disasters such as hurricanes and tsunamis. We've seen what happens to one large city when things break down in the aftermath of Katrina.

In the end, *The Year When Stardust Fell* is just a novel, but the themes it explores continue to have relevance to our modern world.

About the Author
(Note: This text is from the original publication)

At various times, Raymond F. Jones has lived in Utah, Nevada, Arizona, New Mexico and Texas, thereby enabling him to describe the mountain-west community, which is the scene of his newest science fiction book, with sureness and insight. He also has a rich scientific background, which includes training in the fields of radio operating, and electronic engineering, followed by meteorological work with the United States Weather Bureau. To this kaleidoscope of places and things, Mr. Jones has added another facet, that of "a spare-time writer" and has managed to produce eight books, something over one hundred magazine stories, articles and novelettes. This is his third Winston book.

The author was born in Salt Lake City where he is presently living, and attended the University of Utah. He is now working as a researcher with a historical society which possesses the world's largest collection of microfilm copies of ancient documents and records. These documents have been gathered from all parts of Europe and the United States, and Mr. Jones is enjoying this new environment.

Mr. Jones describes the theme of *The Year When Stardust Fell* in this way: "It is the portrayal of the unending conflict between ignorance and superstition on one hand, and knowledge and cultural enlightenment on the other as they come into conflict with each other during an unprecedented disaster brought on by the forces of nature."

Coinciding with the surge of interest in all of science, this book will give the reader a real appreciation of the role of the scientist.

Greg Fowlkes
Editor-In-Chief
Resurrected Press
www.ResurrectedPress.com

PREFACE -
OF MEN OF SCIENCE

The story of man is the story–endlessly repeated–of a struggle: between light and darkness, between knowledge and ignorance, between good and evil, between men who would build and men who would destroy. It is no more complicated than this.

That light, knowledge, good, and constructive men have had a small edge in this struggle is attested to by our slow rise over the long millennia of time. In taking stock of our successes, however, it is easy to assume the victory has been won. Nothing could be further from the truth. This is a contest that is never ended, nor can it be, as long as men are upon the Earth.

While man has free choice, the elements of darkness, ignorance, evil and destruction are available for him to choose, and there are times when these seem the best alternatives.

At the end of the 18th century one of the greatest minds of all time was destroyed by one stroke of a guillotine blade. The judge who presided at the trial of the great French chemist Lavoisier is reported to have said, "The Republic has no need of men of science."

Choices like this have often been made by the society of man. A turnoff to darkness has been deliberately taken, superstition has been embraced while knowledge has been destroyed.

When times are placid we assume such choices could result only from some great insanity; that the men who made them had themselves known more pleasant days. The truth is that there are extremes of circumstance which could force almost any man to abandon that which he has always held to be right and good, and only the very giants could stand up and prove themselves unmoved.

Such giants may seem, in ordinary life, rather obscure. Illustrating this are the people in this story: a somewhat pompous little mayor; a professor of chemistry in a small-town college in the mountain west; a minister of the gospel, who would be lost with a big-city congregation; a sheriff who doesn't care what happens to him personally as long as he sticks to the kind of rightness that has always worked; and a high-school boy who learns what it means to do a man's work.

Such people are important, the most important people alive today. They are the ones whose hands hold all that our culture has achieved when catastrophe overtakes us.

The illusion of security is a vicious one. With physical comforts around us, the abyss that is just beyond our walls is forgotten: the abyss of outer space, beyond the paper-thin atmosphere shielding us; of the fires in the earth beneath; of the hurricane winds beyond the horizon; of the evil and insanity in the minds of many men.

The caveman dared not forget these abysses, nor the frontiersman, nor the scientist who fought the witch hunters to bring forth a new truth of Nature. But when we believe we are secure we do forget them.

In catastrophe, the most recent achievements of the race are the first to go. When war comes, or mobs attack, or hurricanes strike, our science and our arts are abandoned first. Necessity of survival seems to insist that we cannot fool with things of the mind and of the soul when destruction threatens the body. And so, "The Republic has no need of men of science."

Emergency can take any form. Here is a story in which the mechanical foundation of our culture is threatened. Whether the means of this threat, as I have pictured it, could possibly occur, I do not know. I know of no reason why it could not, if circumstances were right.

But more important, this is what happens to a small, college town caught up in such disaster. How quickly do its people dispense with their men of science and turn to superstition and mob rule for hope of survival?

It is perhaps not so apparent to those of us who have grown up with it, but we have witnessed in our own time, under threat of calamity, the decline of science before a blight of crash-priority engineering technology. Today, we hear it faintly whispered, "The Republic has no need of men of science."

Insofar as he represents the achievements of our race over the great reaches of time, the scientist will always be needed if we are to retain the foothold we have gained over Nature. The witch doctors and the fortunetellers clamor for his niche and will gladly extend their services if we wish to change our allegiance.

The story of *The Year When Stardust Fell* is not a story of the distant future or of the remote past. It is not a story of a never-never land where fantastic happenings take place daily. It is a story of my town and yours, of people like you and me and the mayor in townhall, his sheriff on the corner, and the professor in the university—a story that happens no later than tomorrow.

R. F. J.

Table Of Contents

The Year When Stardust Fell
Original Cover Illustration by James Heugh
Other Illustrations by Alex Schomburg

1
THE COMET

The comet was the only thing in the whole sky. All the stars were smothered by the light of its copper-yellow flame, and, although the sun had set two hours ago, the Earth was lit as with the glow of a thunderous dawn.

In Mayfield, Ken Maddox walked slowly along Main Street, avoiding collisions with other people whose eyes were fixed on the object in the sky. Ken had spent scores of hours observing the comet carefully, both by naked eye and with his 12-inch reflecting telescope. Still he could not keep from watching it as he picked his way along the street toward the post office.

The comet had been approaching Earth for months, growing steadily to bigger proportions in the sky, but tonight was a very special night, and Mayfield was watching with increased awe and half-dread–as were hundreds of thousands of other communities around the world.

Tonight, the Earth entered the comet's tail, and during the coming winter would be swept continuously by its million-mile spread.

There was no visible change. The astronomers had cautioned that none was to be expected. The Earth had passed through the tails of comets before, although briefly, and none of the inhabitants had been physically aware of the event.

This time there was a difference. As intangible as a mere suspicion, it could yet be felt, and there was the expectancy of the unknown in the air.

Ken prided himself on a scientific attitude, but it was hard not to share the feelings of those around him that something momentous and mysterious was taking place this night. There would be no quick passage this time. Earth would lie within the tail for a period of over four months as they both made their way about the sun.

Such close-lying orbits had never occurred before in the known history of the world.

"It's frightening, isn't it?"

Ken was aware that he had stopped at the edge of a crowd in front of Billings Drugstore, and beside him Maria Larsen was staring intently upward as she spoke.

She was a small, blonde girl with intense blue eyes. Ken smiled confidently and looked down at her. "No," he said. "It's a beautiful thing. It's a kind of miracle that we should be alive when it happened. No human beings have ever seen such a sight before."

Maria shivered faintly. "I wish I could feel that way. Do you think it will get any bigger?"

"Yes. It will not reach its closest approach for over three months, yet. Its approach is very slow so we won't notice much change."

"It is beautiful," Maria agreed slowly, "but, still, it's frightening. I'll be glad when it's gone."

Ken laughed and tucked the girl's arm in his. There was something so disturbingly serious about the Swedish girl, who was spending a year in Mayfield with her parents. Her father, Dr. Larsen, was a visiting professor of chemistry, engaged to teach this season at the State Agricultural College in Mayfield. Ken's own father was head of the chemistry department there.

"Come down to the post office with me to get some stamps," Ken said. "Then I'll drive you home."

"It's closed. You can't get any stamps tonight."

"Maybe the boys in gray haven't been too busy watching the comet to stock the stamp machine. Look out!" He pulled her back quickly as she stepped from the curb. A wheezy car moved past, its driver completely intent on his observation of the comet.

"Old Dad Martin's been trying to wrap that thing around a pole for 25 years," Ken said unhappily. "It looks like he's going to make it tonight!"

Along the street, bystanders whistled at the aged driver, and pedestrians yelled at one another to get out of the way. The car's progress broke, for a moment, the sense of ominous concern that spread over Main Street.

At the post office, Ken found Maria's prediction was right. The stamp machine was empty.

"I have some at home," the girl said. "You're welcome to them."

"I need a lot. Mother's sending out some invitations."

"I'm sure I have enough. Papa says I'm supporting the postal department with all the letters I write to everyone at home in Sweden."

"All right, I'll take you up on it. I'll get skinned if I don't get them. I was supposed to pick them up this afternoon and I forgot all about it."

"I thought I learned good English in the schools in Sweden," said Maria wistfully, "but I don't seem to understand half what you say. This 'skinned'–what does that mean?"

"Nothing you need to worry about," Ken laughed. "If you would teach me English the way you learned it, Miss Rymer would give me a lot better marks in her class."

"Now I think you're making fun of me," said Maria.

"Not me. Believe me, I'm not! Hey, look what's coming down the street! That's old Granny Wicks. I thought she had died a long time ago."

In front of the post office, an ancient white horse drew a light, ramshackle wagon to a halt. From the seat, a small, wizened, old woman looked at the crowd on the street. She dropped the reins in front of her. Her eyes, set deeply in her wrinkled face, were bright and sharp as a bird's, and moved with the same snapping motions.

From both sides of the street the bystanders watched her. Granny Wicks was known to everyone in Mayfield. She was said to have been the first white child born in the valley, almost a hundred years ago. At one time, her horse and wagon were familiar, everyday sights on the streets, but she seldom came to town any more.

Many people, like Ken, had had the vague impression that she was dead.

She appeared lively enough now as she scrambled down from the wagon seat and moved across the sidewalk to the post office steps. She climbed these and stood in front of the doors. Curiously, the crowd watched her.

"Listen to me, you!" she exclaimed suddenly. Her voice was high and shrill, reminding Ken of an angry bird's. Maria looked at him wonderingly, and he shrugged his shoulders.

"Don't ask me what she's up to. She's pulled some corkers in her time."

Granny Wicks looked over the gathering crowd. Then she pointed a bony arm at the glowing comet. "You know what it means," she exclaimed shrilly. "You feel it in your bones, and your hearts quiver with fear. There's death in the sky, and an omen to all the inhabitants of the Earth that destruction awaits men."

She stopped and glared. The laughter that had first greeted her gave way to uneasiness as people glanced at their neighbors, then hastily at the comet, and back to Granny Wicks. Some began moving away in discomfort.

"You're scared to listen, eh?" Granny shrilled at them. "You're afraid to know what's in store! Turn your backs then! Close your ears! You can't change the signs in the heavens!"

A movement in the crowd caught Ken's eye. He saw the stout figure of Sheriff Johnson moving toward the steps. The law officer stepped out in front and approached Granny Wicks.

"Come on now, Granny," said Sheriff Johnson. "You wouldn't want to scare folks out of a good night's sleep, would you?"

"You let me alone, Sam Johnson! I'm saying what I have to say, and nobody's going to stop me. Listen to me, all of you! There's death in Mayfield in the winter that's coming, and spring won't see one man in ten left alive. Remember what I say. The stars have sent their messenger...."

"Okay, Granny, let's go," said the Sheriff. "You've said your piece and scared the daylights out of everybody. You'd better be getting on out to your place before it gets dark. The comet won't light things up all night. How's your supply of wood and coal for the winter, Granny? The boys been getting it in for you?"

"I got plenty, Sam Johnson. More'n I'll need for this winter. Come spring, I won't be around to be needing anything else from anybody. Neither will you!"

The Sheriff watched as the old woman climbed to her wagon seat again. Those standing nearby helped her gently. She took the reins and snapped them at the weary horse.

"Take care of yourself, Granny!" someone called.

Sheriff Johnson stood silently on the steps until the wagon passed out of sight around the corner of the block. Then he moved slowly by Ken and Maria. He smiled grimly at Ken.

"It's bad enough to have that thing hanging up there in the sky without that kind of talk." He glanced up for a moment. "It gives you the willies. Sometimes I wonder, myself, if Granny isn't half-right."

There was a stillness in the street as the people slowly dispersed ahead of the Sheriff. Voices were low, and the banter was gone. The yellow light from the sky cast weird, bobbing shadows on the pavement and against the buildings.

"Shall we go?" Maria asked. "This is giving me—what do you say?—the creeps."

"It's crazy!" Ken exclaimed with a burst of feeling. "It shows what ignorance of something new and strange can do. One feebleminded, old woman can infect a whole crowd with her crazy superstitions, just because they don't know any more about this thing than she does!"

"It's more than that," said Maria quietly. "It's the feeling that people have always had about the world they find themselves in. It doesn't matter how much you know about the ocean and the winds and the tides, there is always a feeling of wonder and fear when you stand on the shore and watch enormous waves pounding the rocks.

"Even if you know what makes the thunder and the lightning, you can't watch a great storm without feeling very small and puny."

"Of course not," Ken said. "Astronomers feel all that when they look a couple of billion light-years into space. Physicists know it when they discover a new particle of matter. But *they* don't go around muttering about omens and signs. You can feel the strength of natural forces without being scared to death.

"Maybe that's what marks the only real difference between witches and scientists, after all! The first scientist was the guy who saw fire come down from the sky and decided that was the answer to some of his problems. The witch doctor was too scared of both the problem and the answer to believe the problem could ever have a solution. So he manufactured delusions to make himself and others think the problem would just quietly go away. There are a lot of witch doctors still operating and they're not all as easy to recognize as Granny Wicks!"

They reached Ken's car, and he held the door open for Maria. As he climbed in his own side he said, "How about coming over to my place and having a look at the comet through my telescope? You'll see something really awe-inspiring then."

"I'd love to. Right now?"

"Sure." Ken started the car and swung away from the curb, keeping a careful eye on the road, watching for any others like Dad Martin.

"Sometimes I think there will be a great many things I'll miss when we go back to Sweden," Maria said thoughtfully, as she settled back in the seat, enjoying the smooth, powerful ride of Ken's souped-up car.

Ken shot a quick glance at her. He felt a sudden sense of loss, as if he had not realized before that their acquaintance was strictly temporary. "I guess a lot of people here will miss the Larsens, too," he said quietly. "What will you miss most of all?"

"The bigness of everything," said Maria. "The hundreds and hundreds of miles of open country. The schoolboys with cars to cover the distance. At home, a grown man is fortunate to have one. Papa had a very hard time owning one."

"Why don't you persuade him to stay here? Mayfield's a darn good place to live."

"I've tried already, but he says that when a man is grown he has too many things to hold him to the place he's always known. He has promised, however, to let me come back if I want to, after I finish the university at home."

"That would be nice." Ken turned away, keeping his eyes intently on the road. There was nothing else he could say.

He drove slowly up the long grade of College Avenue. His family lived in an older house a block below the brow of College Hill. It gave a pleasant view of the entire expanse of the valley in which Mayfield was situated. The houses of the town ranged themselves in neat, orderly rows below, and spread out on the other side of the business section. In the distance, north and south, were the small farms where hay and dairy stock and truck crops had been raised since pioneer times.

"I'll miss this, too," said Maria. "It's beautiful."

Ken wasn't listening to her, however. The car had begun to sputter painfully as it took the curve leading off the avenue to Linwood Street where Ken lived. He glanced at the heat indicator. The needle was almost at the boiling point.

"For Pete's sake! The water must have leaked out of the radiator."

Ken pulled the car to the curb in front of the house and got out, leaving the engine idling. He raised the hood and cautiously turned the radiator cap with his handkerchief. A cloud of steam shot out, but when he lifted the cap the water was not quite boiling, and there was plenty of it.

Maria came up beside him. "Is something wrong?"

"You've got me there. The radiator's clean. The pump isn't more than two months old. I checked the timing last Saturday. Something's gone sour to make her heat up like that."

From across the street, his neighbor, Mr. Wilkins, approached with a grin. "Looks like the same thing hit us both. Mine started boiling as I came up the hill tonight. It's got me stumped."

"The circulation must be clogged," said Ken. "Either that or the timing has slipped off. That's all it could be."

"Those were my ideas, too. Both wrong in my case. Let me know if you get any other bright ones." He moved off with a pleasant wave of his hand.

"It will cool," said Ken to Maria. "By the time you're ready to leave I'll be able to drive you home."

"I wouldn't want you to damage your car. I can walk."

"We'll see."

He led her around the house. In the center of the backyard loomed the high, round dome of his amateur observatory. It was Ken's personal pride, as well as that of the members of the Mayfield High Science Club, who had helped build the shell and the mountings. The club used it every Thursday night when the seeing was good.

Ken had ground the precision mirror alone. He had ground his first one, a 4-inch glass, when he was a Boy Scout. Three years later he had tackled the tremendous job of producing a 12-inch one. Professor Douglas of the physics department at the college had pronounced it perfect.

Ken opened the door and switched on the light inside the dome. "Don't mind the mess," he said. "I've been taking photographs of the comet for the last month."

To Maria, who was used to the clutter of a laboratory, there was no mess. She admired the beauty of the instrument Ken and his friends had built. "Our university telescope isn't any better," she said.

"You can't tell by the plumbing," Ken laughed. "Better take a look at the image before you pass judgment."

Skilfully, he swung the long tube around to the direction of the comet. With the fine controls he centered the cross hairs of the eyepiece on the blazing object in the sky.

"It's moving too fast to stay in range very long," he said.

Maria stepped to the observer's position. She gasped suddenly at the image of the fiery monster hovering in the sky. Viewing the comet along the axis of the tail, as the Earth lay at the edge of it, an observer's vision was like that of a miniature, flaming sun with an offcenter halo of pulsing, golden light.

To Maria, the comet seemed like something living. Slow, almost imperceptible ripples in the glowing scarves of light made them sway as if before some mighty, cosmic wind in space.

"It's beautiful," Maria murmured, "but it's terrible, too. No wonder the ancients believed comets brought evil and death upon the Earth. I could almost believe it, myself!"

2
BREAKDOWN

Ken Maddox could not remember a time when he had not wanted to become a scientist. Maybe it started when his father first invited him to look through a microscope. That was when he was a very small boy, but he could still remember the revelation of that experience. He remembered how it had seemed, on looking away from the lens, that the whole world of normal vision was only a fragment of that which was hidden behind curtains and shrouds and locked doors. Only men, like his father, with special instruments and wisdom and knowledge, could ever hope to understand the world of the unknown, which the ordinary person did not even suspect.

Now, at sixteen, Ken was tall, with black hair that had an annoying curl to it. He was husky enough to be the main asset of the football squad of Mayfield High School in his senior year. He knew exactly where he was going and what he was going to do. He would be one of those men who lived beyond the mere surface of the world, and who would seek to understand its deep and hidden meanings.

Ken thought of this as he watched Maria at the telescope. What a difference between knowing the comet as this instrument showed it, and with the knowledge revealed by modern astronomy, and knowing it as the average person in Mayfield did.

Ken and Maria stayed in the observatory until the comet had almost disappeared below the horizon. Mrs. Maddox brought a snack of sandwiches and punch.

"I always do this when I see the observatory dome open," she said, smiling. "I never know when Ken's going to quit his stargazing and come in for the night."

"We're about through, Mom. I'll drive Maria over to her place and be back in a little while."

"I'm going to loan him the stamps," Maria said.

Mrs. Maddox looked at Ken in mock severity. "You mean you forgot *again*?"

"No–I remembered," Ken said lamely. "After the post office closed, that is. Anyhow, Maria has plenty."

"Well," said Mrs. Maddox, "I know who's going to have to mail my invitations if they're ever to get out in time for the party!"

After he and Maria had finished the snack, Ken started his car again. The engine had cooled to normal temperature, but he watched the indicator closely as he drove. Nothing seemed right about the action of the car. The engine had turned over sluggishly when he pressed the starter button, as if the battery were almost dead. Now it lugged heavily, even when going downhill.

"The whole thing's haywire," Ken said irritably. "It acts like the crankcase is full of sand or something."

"Let me walk the rest of the way," said Maria. "You take the car back, and I'll bring the stamps over on my way to school in the morning."

"No, we're almost there. Nothing much more could go wrong than already has."

When they reached Maria's place they found Professor and Mrs. Larsen sitting on the porch.

"We've been watching the comet," Maria said excitedly. "Ken let me look at it through his telescope."

"A remarkable event," said Professor Larsen. "I feel very fortunate to be alive to witness it. My generation hasn't had this kind of privilege before. I was a child when Halley's comet appeared."

"I've been trying to tell Maria what a lucky break this is, but she agrees with Granny Wicks," said Ken.

"Oh, I do not!" Maria snapped.

"Granny Wicks?" Professor Larsen inquired. "Your grandmother?"

"No." Ken tried to cover the professor's lack of familiarity with American idioms. "She's just the town's oldest citizen. Everybody likes her and calls her Granny, but her mind belongs to the Middle Ages."

"You hear that, Papa?" cried Maria. "Her mind belongs to the Middle Ages, and he says I'm like Granny Wicks!"

Maria's mother laughed gently. "I'm sure Ken didn't mean your mind is of the Middle Ages, too, dear."

Ken flushed. "Of course not. What I mean is that Granny Wicks thinks the comet is something mysterious and full of omens, and Maria says she sort of thinks the same about it."

"I didn't say anything about omens and signs!"

"Well, except for that...."

"Except for that, I suppose we are all in agreement," said Professor Larsen slowly. He drew on his pipe and it glowed brightly in the darkness. "The whole universe is a terrible place that barely tolerates living organisms. Almost without exception it is filled with great suns that are flaming, atomic furnaces, or dead cinders of planets to which a scrap of poisonous atmosphere may cling. Yes, it is indeed a great miracle that here in this corner of the universe conditions exist where living things have found a foothold. We may be glad that this is so, but it does not pay man to ever forget the fierceness of the home in which he lives. Earth is merely one room of that home, on the pleasant, sunny side of the house. But the whole universe is his home."

"That's the thing I've been trying to say," Ken answered. "We can know this without being afraid."

Maria's father nodded. "Yes. Fear is of no use to anyone. Awe, respect, admiration, wonder, humility—these are all necessary. But not fear."

Maria turned from the group. "I'll bring the stamps, Ken," she said.

"Won't you come in and have some cake?" Mrs. Larsen asked.

"No, thanks. Mother fed us before we left my place. I'm afraid I couldn't eat any more."

In a moment Maria was back. "Here are two whole sheets," she said. "I hope that will be enough."

"Plenty. I'll see you get repaid tomorrow. Good night, everybody."

"Good night, Ken."

He moved down the walk toward his car and got in. When he pressed die starter button the engine groaned for a few seconds and came to a complete stop. He tried again; there was only a momentary, protesting grind.

Ken got out and raised the hood and leaned over the engine in disgusted contemplation. There was no visible clue to the cause of the trouble.

"Is your battery dead?" Professor Larsen called.

"No. It's something else." Ken slammed the hood harder than he had intended. "I'll have to leave it here overnight and pick it up in the morning."

"I can push you home with my car, or at least give you a ride."

"No, please don't bother," Ken said. "I'll tow it home with Dad's car tomorrow. I'd just as soon walk, now. It's only a few blocks."

"As you wish. Good night, Ken."

"Good night, Professor."

*   *   *   *   *

Ken's clock radio woke him the next morning. He reached over to shut off the newscast it carried. There was only one item any commentator talked about now, the comet. Ken wondered how they could get away with a repetition of the same thing, over and over, but they seemed able to get an audience as long as they kept the proper tone of semi-hysteria in their voices.

As his hand touched the dial to switch it off, something new caught Ken's attention. "A curious story is coming in from all parts of the country this morning," the announcer said. "Auto mechanics are reporting a sudden, unusually brisk business. No one knows the reason, but there seems to be a virtual epidemic of car breakdowns. Some garagemen are said to be blaming new additives in gasoline and lubricating oil. It is reported that one major oil company is undertaking an investigation of these charges, but, in the meantime, no one really seems to have a good answer.

"In connection with the comet, however, from widely scattered areas comes the report that people are even blaming these engine failures on our poor, old comet. In the Middle Ages they blamed comets for everything from soured cream to fallen kingdoms. Maybe this modern age isn't so different, after all. At any rate, this comet will no doubt be happy to get back into open space, where there are no Earthmen to blame it for all their accidents and shortcomings!"

Ken switched off the radio and lay back on the pillow. That was a real choice one—blaming the comet for car breakdowns! Page Granny Wicks!

The breakdowns were curious, however. There was no good reason why there should be a sudden rash of them. He wondered if they had actually occurred, or if the story was just the work of some reporter trying to make something out of his own inability to get into a couple of garages that were swamped by the usual weekend rush. This was most likely the case.

However it didn't explain why his own car had suddenly conked out, Ken thought irritably. He'd have to get it over to Art Matthews' garage as soon as school was out.

At school that morning there was little talk of anything but the comet. After physics class, Ken was met by Joe Walton and three other members of the science club, of which Ken was president.

"We want a special meeting," said Joe. "We've just had the most brilliant brainstorm of our brief careers."

"It had better be more brilliant than the last one," said Ken. "That drained the club treasury of its last peso."

"I was watching the comet last night, and I began to smell the dust of its tail as the Earth moved into it...."

"You must have been smelling something a lot more powerful than comet dust."

"I said to myself—why don't we collect some of that stuff and bottle it and see what it's made of? What do you think?" Joe asked eagerly.

Ken scowled. "Just how many molecules of material from the comet's tail do you think there are in the atmosphere over Mayfield right now?"

"How do I know? Six—maybe eight."

Ken laughed. "You're crazy, anyway. What have you got in mind?"

"I'm not sure," Joe answered seriously. "We know the comet's tail is so rarefied that it resembles a pretty fair vacuum, but it *is* composed of something. As it mixes with the atmosphere we ought to be able to determine the changing makeup of the air and get a pretty good idea of the composition of the comet's tail. This is a chance nobody's ever had before—and maybe never will again, until we go right out there in spaceships—being right inside a comet's tail long enough to analyze it!"

"It sounds like a terrific project," Ken admitted. "The universities will all be doing it, of course, but it would still be a neat trick if we could bring it off. Maybe Dad and Professor Larsen will have ideas on how we could do it."

"We ought to be able to make most of the equipment," said Joe, "so it shouldn't be too expensive. Anyway, we'll have a meeting then, right after school?"

"Yes–no, wait. The engine in my car conked out. I've got to go over to Art's with it this afternoon. You go ahead without me. Kick the idea around and let me know what's decided. I'll go along with anything short of mortgaging the football field."

"Okay," said Joe. "I don't see why you don't just sell that hunk of junk and get a real automobile. You've got a good excuse now. This breakdown is a good omen!"

"Don't talk to me about omens!"

*   *   *   *   *

Art Matthews had the best equipped garage in town, and was a sort of unofficial godfather to all the hot-rodders in the county. He helped them plane the heads of their cars. He got their special cams and carburetor and manifold assemblies wholesale, and he gave them fatherly advice about using their heads when they were behind the wheel.

Ken called him at noon. "I've got troubles, Art," he said. "Can I bring the car over after school?"

"I'm afraid I can't do a thing for you today," Art Matthews said. "I don't know what's happened, but I've had tow calls all day. Right now the shop is full and they're stacked four-high outside. I'm going to do a couple of highway patrol cars and Doc Adams'. I figured they ought to have priority."

Ken felt a sudden, uneasy sense of recognition. This was the same kind of thing he had heard about on the radio that morning! A rash of car breakdowns all over the country. Now, the same thing in Mayfield!

"What's wrong with them?" he asked the mechanic. "Why is everybody coming in with trouble at the same time?"

"They're not coming in," said Art. "I'm having to go out after them. I don't know yet what's wrong. They heat up and stall. It's the craziest thing I've run into in 30 years of garage work."

"Mine acted the same way," Ken said.

"Yeah? Well, you're in good company. Listen, why don't you and maybe Joe and Al come down and give me a hand after school? I'll never get on top here without some help. After we get these police and other priority cars out of the way, maybe we can get a quick look at what's wrong with yours."

"It's a deal."

Joe Walton wasn't much in favor of spending that afternoon and an unknown number of others in Art's garage; he was too overwhelmed by the idea of analyzing the material of the comet's tail. However Art had done all of them too many favors in the past to ignore his call for help.

"The trouble with this town," Joe said, "is that three-fourths of the so-called automobiles running around the streets belong down at Thompson's Auto Wrecking."

Al Miner agreed to come, too. When they reached the garage after school they saw Art had not been exaggerating. His place was surrounded by stalled cars, and the street outside was lined with them in both directions. Ken borrowed the tow truck and brought his own car back from the Larsens'. By that time the other two boys were at work.

"Batteries are all okay," Art told him. "Some of these engines will turn over, but most of them won't budge. I've jerked a couple of heads, but I can't see anything. I want you to take the pans off and take down the bearings to see if they're frozen. That's what they act like. When that's done, we'll take it from there."

Ken hoisted the front end of one of the police cars and slid under it on a creeper. Art's electric impact wrenches were all in use, so he began the laborious removal of the pan bolts by hand. He had scarcely started when he heard a yell from Joe who was beneath the other police car.

"What's the matter?" Art called.

"Come here! Look at this!"

The others crowded around, peering under the car. Joe banged and pried at one of the bearings, still clinging to the crankshaft after the cap had been removed.

"Don't do that!" Art shouted at him. "You'll jimmy up the crankshaft!"

"Mr. Matthews," Joe said solemnly, "this here crankshaft has been jimmied up just as much as it's ever going to get jimmied. These bearings are welded solid. They'll have to be machined off!"

"Nothing could freeze them to the shaft that hard," Art exclaimed.

Joe moved out of the way. Art crawled under and tapped the bearing. He pried at it with a chisel. Then he applied a cold chisel and pounded. The bearing metal came away chip by chip, but the bulk of it clung to the shaft as if welded.

"I've never seen anything like that before in my life!" Art came out from beneath the car.

"What do you think could cause it?" Joe asked.

"Gas!" said Art vehemently. "The awful gas they're putting out these days. They put everything into it except sulphur and molasses, and they expect an engine to run. Additives, they call 'em! Detergents! Why can't they sell us plain old gasoline?"

Ken watched from a distance behind the group. He looked at the silent, motionless cars in uneasy speculation. He recalled again the radio announcement of that morning. Maybe it *could* be something they were adding to the gas or oil, as Art said. It couldn't, however, happen so suddenly—not all over the country. Not in New York, Montgomery, Alabama, San Francisco, and Mayfield. Not all at the same time.

Art turned up the shop lights. Outside, as the sun lowered in the sky, the glow of the comet began turning the landscape a copper-yellow hue. Its light came through the broad doors of the garage and spread over the half-dismantled cars.

"All right, let's go," said Art. His voice held a kind of false cheeriness, as if something far beyond his comprehension had passed before him and he was at a loss to meet it or even understand it.

"Let's go," he said again. "Loosen all those connecting rods and get the shafts out. We'll see what happens when we try to pull the pistons."

3
POWER FAILURE

The news broadcasts the following morning were less hysterical than previously. Because the news itself was far more serious, the announcers found it unnecessary to inject artificial notes of urgency.

Ken listened to his bedside radio as he watched the first tint of dawn above the hills east of the valley. "The flurry of mechanical failures, which was reported yesterday, has reached alarming proportions," the announcer said. "During the past 24 hours garages in every section of the nation have been flooded with calls. From the other side of the Atlantic reports indicate the existence of a similar situation in Europe and in the British Isles.

"Automobile breakdowns are not the most serious accidents that are taking place. Other forms of machinery are also being affected. A crack train of the Southern Pacific came to a halt last night in the Arizona desert. All efforts of the crew to repair the stalled engine were fruitless. A new one had to be brought up in order for the passengers to continue on their way early this morning.

"From Las Vegas comes word that one of the huge generators at Hoover Dam has been taken out of service because of mechanical failure. Three other large municipalities have had similar service interruptions. These are Rochester, New York, Clinton, Missouri, and Bakersfield, California.

"Attempts have been made to find some authoritative comment on the situation from scientists and Government officials. So far, no one has been willing to commit himself to an opinion as to the cause of this unexplained and dangerously growing phenomenon.

"Yesterday it was jokingly whispered that the comet was responsible. Today, although no authority can be found to verify it, the rumor persists that leading scientists are seriously considering the possibility that the comet may actually have something to do with the breakdowns."

Ken turned off the radio and lay back with his hands beneath his head, staring at the ceiling. His first impulse was to ridicule again this fantastic idea about the comet. Yet, there had to be *some* explanation.

He had seen enough of the engines in Art's garage last night to know they had suffered no ordinary mechanical disorder. Something had happened to them that had never happened to engines before, as far as he knew. The crankshafts were immovable in their bearings. The pistons had been frozen tight in the cylinders when they tried to remove some of them. Every moving part was welded to its mating piece as solidly as if the whole engine had been heated to the very edge of melting and then allowed to cool.

Apparently something similar was happening to engines in every part of the world. It could only mean that some common factor was at work in London, and Paris, and Cairo, and Mayfield. The only such factor newly invading the environment of every city on the globe was the comet.

It would almost require a belief in witchcraft to admit the comet might be responsible!

Ken arose and dressed slowly. By the time he was finished he heard his father's call to breakfast from downstairs.

Professor Maddox was already seated when Ken entered the dining room. He was a tall, spare man with an appearance of intense absorption in everything about him.

He glanced up and nodded a pleasant good morning as Ken approached. "I hear you worked overtime as an auto mechanic last night," he said. "Isn't that a bit rough, along with the load you're carrying at school?"

"Art asked us to do him a favor. Haven't you seen what's been happening around town?"

"I noticed an unusual number of cars around the garage, and I wondered about it. Has everyone decided to take care of their winter repairs at the same time?"

"Haven't you heard the radio, either, Dad?"

"No. I've been working on my new paper for the *Chemical Journal* until midnight for the last week. What has the radio got to do with your work as a mechanic?"

Quickly, Ken outlined to his father the events he had heard reported the past two days. "It's not only automobiles, but trains, power plants, ships, everything—"

Professor Maddox looked as if he could scarcely believe Ken was not joking. "That would certainly be a strange set of coincidences," he said finally, "provided the reports are true, of course."

"It's true, all right," said Ken. "It's not a matter of coincidence. Something is causing it to happen!"

"What could that possibly be?"

"There's talk about the comet having something to do with it."

Professor Maddox almost choked on his spoonful of cereal. "Ken," he laughed finally, "I thought you were such a stickler for rigid, scientific methods and hypotheses! What's happened to all your rigor?"

Ken looked down at the tablecloth. "I know it sounds ridiculous, like something out of the dim past, when they blamed comets for corns, and broken legs, and lost battles. Maybe this time it isn't so crazy when you stop to think about it, and it's absolutely the only new factor which could have some worldwide effect."

"How could it have any effect at all—worldwide or otherwise?" Professor Maddox demanded.

"The whole world is immersed in its tail."

"And that tail is so tenuous that our senses do not even detect the fact!"

"That doesn't mean it couldn't have some kind of effect."

"Such as stopping engines? Well, you're a pretty good mechanic. Just what did the comet do to all these stalled pieces of machinery?"

Ken felt his father was being unfair, yet he could scarcely blame him for not taking the hypothesis seriously. "I don't know what the comet did—or could do—" he said in a low voice. "I just know I've never seen any engines like those we took apart last night."

In detail, he described to his father the appearance of the engine parts they had dismantled. "I brought home some samples of metal we cut from the engine blocks with a torch. Would you take them up to the laboratory at the college and have them examined under the electron microscope?"

"I wouldn't have time to run any such tests for several days. If you are intent on pursuing this thing, however, I'll tell you what I'll do. You and your science club friends can come up and use the equipment yourselves."

"We don't know how!"

"I'll arrange for one of the teaching fellows to show you how to prepare metallic samples and operate the electron microscope."

Ken's eyes lighted. "Gee, that would be great if you would do that, Dad! Will you, really?"

"Come around after school today. I'll see that someone is there to help you."

Art Matthews was disappointed when Ken called and said none of the science club members would be around that afternoon. He couldn't keep from showing in his voice that he felt they were letting him down.

"It's not any use trying to get those engines running," Ken said. "The pistons would never come out of most of them without being drilled out. We're not equipped for that. Even if we got things loosened up and running again, what would keep the same thing from happening again? That's what we've got to find out."

Art was unable to accept this point of view. He held a bewildered but insistent belief that something ought to be done about the mounting pile of disabled cars outside his garage. "We can get some of them going, Ken. You fellows have got to lend a hand. I can't tackle it without help."

"I'm sorry," Ken said. "We're convinced there's got to be another way to get at the problem."

"All right. You guys do whatever you figure you've got to do. I can probably round up some other help."

Ken hung up, wishing he had been able to make Art understand, but the mechanic would probably be the last person in Mayfield to accept that the comet could have any possible connection with the frozen engines.

As Ken walked to school that morning he estimated that at least 25 percent of the cars in Mayfield must be out of commission. Some of the men in his neighborhood were in their driveways futilely punching their starters while their engines moaned protestingly or refused to turn over at all. Others were peering under the hoods, shaking their heads, and calling across the yards to their neighbors.

In the street, some cars were lugging with great difficulty, but others moved swiftly along without any evidence of trouble. Ken wondered how there could be such a difference, and if some might prove immune, so to speak, to the effect.

He had called a meeting of the club in the chemistry laboratory for an hour before the first class. All of the members were there when he arrived.

Ken called the meeting to order at once. "I guess you've all heard the news broadcasts, and you know what's happening here in town," he said. "Yesterday you talked about the possibility of collecting samples and analyzing the material of the comet's tail. I don't know what you decided. You can fill me in later on that. The problem is a lot more important now than it was yesterday.

"It's beginning to seem as if the presence of the comet may actually be responsible for the wave of mechanical failures. Finding out how and why is just about the biggest problem in the whole world right now."

A babble of exclamations and protests arose immediately from the other members of the group. Al Miner and Dave Whitaker were on their feet. Ted Watkins waved a hand and shouted, "Don't tell us you're swallowing that superstitious junk!"

Ken held up a hand. "One at a time. We haven't got all day, and there's a lot of ground to cover. Ted, what's your comment?"

"My comment is that anybody's got a screw loose if he believes the comet's got anything to do with all those cars being in Art's garage. That stuff went out of fashion after the days of old Salem."

Several of the others nodded vigorously as Ted spoke.

"I guess we do need to bring some of you up to date on the background material," said Ken. "Joe, tell them what we found last night."

Briefly, Joe Walton described the engines they had dismantled. "Something had happened to them," he said, "which had never happened to an engine since Ford drove his first horseless carriage down Main Street."

"It doesn't mean anything!" exclaimed Ted. "No matter what it is, we haven't any basis for tying it to the comet."

"Can you name any other universal factor that could account for it?" Ken asked. "We have an effect that appears suddenly in Mayfield, Chicago, Paris, and Cairo. Some people say it's the additives in gasoline, but you don't get them showing up simultaneously in all parts of the world. There is no other factor common to every locality where the mechanical failures have occurred, except the comet.

"So I called this meeting to suggest that we expand our project beyond anything we previously had in mind. I suggest we try to determine the exact relationship between the breakdowns and the appearance of the comet."

Big Dave Whitaker, sitting at the edge of the room, rose slowly in his seat. "You've got the cart before the horse," he said. "You've got a nice theory all set up and you want us to beat our brains out trying to prove it. Now, take me. I've got a theory that little green men from Mars have landed and are being sucked into the air intake of the engines. Prove my theory first, why don't you?"

Ken grinned good-naturedly. "I stand corrected, but I won't back down very far. I won't suggest we try to prove the connection with the comet, but I do propose to set up some experiments to discover if there is any relationship. If there is, then what it is. Does that suit you?"

"I'll go along with that. How do you propose to go about it?"

"Let's find out where the rest stand," said Ken. "How about it, you guys?"

"I'll go for it," said Ted, "as long as we aren't out to prove a medieval superstition."

One by one, the others nodded agreement. Joe Walton said intensely, "We'll find out whether it's superstition or not! There's no other possible cause, and we'll prove it before we're through."

Ken smiled and waved him down. "We're working on a hypothesis only. Anyway, here's what I have to suggest by way of procedure: Since the tail of the comet is so rarefied, there aren't many molecules of it in the atmosphere of this entire valley. I don't know just what the mathematical chances of getting a measurable sample are. Maybe you can work out some figures on it, Dave. We'll have to handle an enormous volume of air, so let's get a blower as large as we can get our hands on and funnel the air through some electrically charged filters. We can wash down these filters with a solvent of some kind periodically and distill whatever has collected on them."

"You won't get enough to fill the left eye of a virus suffering from arrested development," said Ted.

"We'll find out when we get set up," said Ken. "My father has agreed to give us access to the electron microscope at the college. Maybe we can use their new mass spectrograph to help analyze whatever we collect."

"If we knew how to use a mass spectrograph," said Ted.

"He's offered to let one of the teaching fellows help us."

"What will all this prove, even if we do find something?" Dave asked. "You'll get all kinds of lines from a spectrogram of atmospheric dust. So what?"

"If we should get some lines that we can't identify, and if we should get those same lines from metallic specimens taken from the disabled engines, we would have evidence of the presence of a new factor. Then we could proceed with a determination of what effect, if any, this factor has on the engines."

Ken looked around the group once more. "Any comments, suggestions, arguments? There being none, we'll consider the project approved, and get to work this afternoon."

As they left to go to their first classes, Ted shook his head gloomily. "Man, you don't know what you're biting off! All we've done so far is build a few ham radios, a telescope, and some Geiger counters. You're talking about precision work now, and I mean *pree*-cision!"

Throughout the day Ken, too, felt increasing doubts about their ability to carry off the project. It would be a task of tremendous delicacy to analyze such microscopic samples as they might succeed in obtaining. Microchemical methods would be necessary, and none of them had had any experience in that field. His father was an expert with these methods and though he might scold them for tackling such a difficult project, he'd help them, Ken thought. He always had.

This was no ordinary project, however. Ken had no idea how seriously scientists in general were considering the comet as the offender, but certainly they must be working frantically on the problem of the mechanical disorder. Unless they found another cause very soon, they were certain to turn to an analysis of the comet's tail. It would be very satisfying if Ken's group could actually be in the vanguard of such a development.

He tried to ridicule his own conviction that the comet held the key. He had no reason whatever for such a belief, except the fact of the comet's universal presence. How it could stop an automobile engine or a railroad train was beyond his wildest imaginings.

But there was nothing else. Nothing at all.

On the way home after school, there seemed to Ken to be a subtle change that had come over the valley since morning. Along the streets, cars were parked in front of houses to which they did not belong. Little knots of people were standing about, talking in hushed tones. The comet was aflame in the sky.

There seemed to be not merely an awe and an uneasiness in the people, but a genuine fear that Ken could not help absorbing as he moved past them on the sidewalks. Their faces were yellow and flat under the glare of the comet, and they looked at him and at each other as if they were strangers in an alien land.

Almost without being aware of it, Ken found himself running the last half-block before he reached his own home. He burst in the door and called out with forced cheeriness, "Hi, Mom, what's cooking? I'm starved. The whole gang's coming over in a few minutes. I hope you've got something for them."

His mother came out of the kitchen, her face gray with uncertainty. "You'll have to do with sandwiches this afternoon," she said. "I haven't been able to use the electric stove since noon."

Ken stared at her.

"There's something about the power," she went on. "We haven't any lights, either. They say the power station at Collin's Dam went out of commission this morning. They don't know when they'll be able to get it back on."

4
DISASTER SPREADS

While he stood, shocked by his mother's statement, Ken heard the phone ringing in the next room. On battery power at the telephone central office, he thought.

His mother answered, and there was a pause. "Professor Maddox is at the college," she said. "You can probably reach him there, or I can give him your message when he comes home."

She returned to the doorway. "That was the power company. They want your father and Dr. Douglas to have a look at their generators.

"Ken, what do you think this means?" she asked worriedly. "What will happen if all our power goes off and doesn't come back on? Do you think your father has any idea what's causing the trouble?"

Ken shook his head. "I don't know, Mom. So far, nobody seems to know anything."

In less than 15 minutes, Professor Maddox hurried into the house. "Couldn't get my car going," he said. "It's stalled on the campus parking lot. The power company wants me to go to Collin's Dam."

"I know," said Mrs. Maddox. "They called here."

He paused a moment, staring out the window, a look of bewilderment on his face. "This thing seems to be more serious than I would have believed possible. There's just no explanation for it, none at all!"

"Any chance of my going along, Dad?" Ken said.

"I'm afraid not. We're going in Dr. Larsen's car, and it's half loaded with instruments. I hope we make it there and back without breaking down.

"I'll probably be back early this evening, but don't hold dinner on my account."

"There will be only sandwiches," said Ken's mother. "I can't cook anything."

"Of course. Just leave me some of whatever you have."

From the doorway Ken watched his father and the other two scientists. He thought he detected a loginess in the engine as Professor Larsen drove away from the curb.

What they hoped to accomplish, Ken didn't know, but he felt certain they would find the same thing in the generators that had been found in the automobile engines. The bearings were probably frozen so tight that they and the shaft had become one solid piece of metal. He hoped the scientists would bring back some samples of the metal.

By 4 o'clock all the members of the science club had arrived. They met in what Ken called his "science shack," a small building next to the observatory. Here he kept the amateur radio equipment belonging to the club, and his own personal collections in the several different fields in which he had been interested since his Boy Scout days.

In each of his companions, Ken could see the effect of the feeling that now pervaded the town. Their usual horseplay was almost forgotten, and their faces were sober to the point of fear.

"We aren't going to be able to run our blower by electricity," said Joe Walton. "We can't even get power for the precipitating filters."

"Let's scrounge anything we can find that runs on gasoline or coal oil," said Al Miner. "If we act fast we ought to be able to pick up some old motorcycle engines or some power lawn mowers from the dump. Thompson's have probably got some. We can try people's basements, too. Let's get as many as possible, because we don't know how long any one will last, and we may have to run the blower for weeks, in order to get any kind of sample."

"Good idea," said Ken. "Here's something else: Who's got a car left to gather this stuff in?"

The boys looked at each other.

"Ours was still running this morning," Frank Abrams said, "but I won't guarantee how long we can count on it."

"Pretty soon there won't be any we can count on. We've got to get a horse and wagon before they start selling for as much as a new Cadillac used to."

"My uncle's got one on his farm," said Dave Whitaker. "He would probably loan it to me, but he's five miles out of town."

"Take my bike," said Ken. "See if he'll let you borrow it and a wagon for at least a couple of weeks or longer. Bring some bales of hay, too."

"Right now?"

"Right now."

When Dave had gone, Al said, "What about the blower? Anybody know where we can get one of those?"

"I think there's one at Thompson's," said Ted. "They pulled it out of Pete and Mary's restaurant when they remodeled."

"That would be just a little kitchen blower. Not big enough—we need a man-sized one."

Ken said, after a long pause, "There isn't one in town. The chances of getting one from somewhere else are practically zero. Frederick is 50 miles away and by tomorrow there may not be a car in town that would go that far."

"Look," said Al, "how about the air-conditioning systems in town? There isn't one that's any good where it is, now. Both the high school and the college have big ones. I'll bet we could get permission at either place to revamp the intake and outlet ducts so we could put in our filters and precipitators. Your father and his friends could swing it for us at the college."

"You might be right! It's worth trying. For precipitators we can rig a battery-powered system that will put a few thousand volts on the screens. Art will let us have enough car batteries for that. I think we're set!"

*   *   *   *   *

Dave Whitaker did not return until dusk, but he had succeeded in getting the horse and wagon, and a load of hay. He deposited this in his own yard before driving back to Ken's place.

During the next two or three hours the boys found two old motorcycle engines, a power lawn-mower motor, and one old gasoline-powered washing machine. All of these they took down to Art Matthews' place and begged him for space and tools to overhaul the equipment.

"You can have the whole joint," Art said dejectedly. "This pile of junk will never move!" He waved a hand at the cars lined up and down both sides of the streets near his place.

By 9 o'clock they had succeeded in getting all of the small engines running, but they dared not test them too long, hoping to conserve all possible life that might be left. When they were through, they returned to Ken's house. Mrs. Maddox had sandwiches ready for them.

No word had been heard from the three scientists who had gone to the power plant. Maria called, anxious about her father.

"I'm worried, Ken," she said. "What would happen to them out there if the car breaks down and they have no place to go?"

"They'll be all right," Ken reassured her. "They probably found something bigger than they expected at the dam. If they should have trouble with the car they can find a phone along the road at some farmhouse and let us know."

"I can't help worrying," said Maria. "Everything feels so strange tonight, just the way it does before a big thunderstorm, as if something terrible were going to happen!"

Ken sensed the way she felt. It was all he could do to hold back the same reaction within himself, but he knew it must be far more difficult for Maria, being in a foreign country among strangers with customs she didn't understand.

"Why don't you and your mother come over here until they get back?" he asked.

"Suppose they don't come back at all? Tonight, I mean."

"Then you can sleep here. Mom's got plenty of room."

"I'll ask Mamma. If it's all right with her, we'll be right over."

Ken hoped they would come. He found himself concerned beyond all reason that Maria and her mother should be made comfortable and relieved of their worries.

He went out to the backyard again, where all the other members of the club were still lounging on the grass, watching the sky. The comet was twenty degrees above the horizon, although the sun had long since set below the western mountains. No one seemed to feel this was a night for sleeping.

"Let's try your battery portable for a few minutes," said Joe Walton. "I'd like to know what's going on in the rest of the world."

Ken brought it out and turned it on. The local station was off the air, of course, and so was the one in Frederick. Half the power there came from the Collin's Dam. More than one-third of the usual stations were missing, but Ken finally picked up one coming in clearly from the northern tip of the state.

The announcer didn't sound like an announcer. He sounded like an ordinary man in the midst of a great and personal tragedy.

"Over three-fourths of the cars in the United States," he was saying, "are now estimated to be out of commission. The truck transportation system of the country has all but broken down. The railroads have likewise suffered from this unbelievable phenomenon.

"All machinery which involves rolling or sliding contact between metal parts has been more or less affected. Those equipped with roller bearings are holding up longer than those equipped with bushings, but all are gradually failing.

"In New York City half the power capacity has gone out of commission. Some emergency units have been thrown into operation, but these cannot carry the load, and even some of them have failed. Elsewhere, across the nation, the story is similar. In Chicago, Kansas City, St. Louis, Washington, San Francisco–the power systems are breaking down along with motor and rail transportation.

"For some hours now, the President and his Cabinet have been in session with dozens of scientific leaders trying to find an explanation and a cure for this disastrous failure of machinery. Rumors which were broadcast widely this morning concerning possible effects of the comet have been thoroughly discredited by these scientists, who call them superstitions belonging back in the Middle Ages.

"One final report has just come over the air by shortwave. In the Atlantic Ocean the Italian steamer *White Bird* has radioed frantically that her engines are dead. Over eight hundred passengers and crew are aboard.

"All ship sailings have been canceled since noon today. Vessels at sea are returning to nearest port. There is no ship available which can take off the stranded passengers and crew of the *White Bird*. She floats helpless and alone tonight in the middle of the Atlantic Ocean.

"As a power-conservation measure, broadcasting on this network will cease until midnight, eastern standard time. Turn your radios off. Keep all unnecessary lights off. Avoid consumption of power in every possible way. Be with us again at midnight for the latest news and information."

There was a restlessness in all of Mayfield. None of the townspeople felt like sleeping that night. Ken's group watched the comet until it disappeared below the horizon. Some of them observed it through the telescope. On either side of the Maddoxes' yard the voices of neighbors could be heard under the night sky, speaking in hushed tones of the thing that had happened.

Maria and Mrs. Larsen arrived, and Maria joined Ken and his friends in the backyard. He told her what they had heard on the radio.

"That ship ..." Maria said slowly. "The *White Bird*, out there alone in the ocean—what will become of all those people?"

Ken shook his head slowly. "There's no way to get to them. There's not a thing that can be done. Nothing at all."

They remained quiet for a long time, as if each were thinking his own thoughts about the mystery and loneliness and death riding the forsaken ship in the middle of the ocean, and how soon it might be that the same dark shadow settled over the cities and towns.

Maria thought of her far-off homeland, and the people she knew, suddenly frightened and helpless in their inability to get power and food.

Ken thought of the scenes that must be occurring in the big cities of the United States. People everywhere would not be sleeping tonight. They were all citizens of a civilization that was dependent for its life on turning wheels and on power surging through bright wires across hundreds of miles of open country. Without those turning wheels, and the power in those wires there was no food, there was no warmth, there was no life.

They listened to the radio again at midnight. There was little that was new. The President's council had found no solution, nor had they come to any decisions. Scattered riots and public disorders were springing up, both in Europe and America. On the high seas, the captain of the *White Bird* was begging for assistance, demanding to know what had happened that no ship could be sent to his aid.

Word finally came from Ken's father and his companions that their car had failed after leaving the dam to return home. They had reached a farmhouse where they would spend the rest of the night. They would try to find some kind of transportation in the morning.

In the early-morning hours Ken's friends drifted away, one by one, to their own homes, and as dawn approached, Ken finally went up to his own room and slept. Maria and her mother, with Ken's mother, had retired only a short time earlier.

When he awoke at 9 o'clock Ken had no idea whether or not the school officials planned to hold classes that day, but he felt that for himself and the other members of the science club there would be no return to normal activity for a long time. Since his father would not return for an indefinite time Ken determined to approach President Lewis of the college regarding the use of the idle blower and ventilation ducts in the Science Hall.

He had met President Lewis a number of times and believed the president would listen to him.

Another matter had disturbed Ken since last night. As soon as he was awake he called the office of Mayor Hilliard. The Mayor's secretary answered and said, "Mayor Hilliard is in conference. He will not be available today."

Ken hesitated. "Tell him it is the Maddox residence calling. I think Mayor Hilliard will answer."

In a moment the Mayor's voice boomed on the phone. Normally hearty, it was now weighted with overtones of uncertainty and fear. "Professor Maddox, I was just about to call you. Would you...."

"This is not Professor Maddox," said Ken. "I'm his son, Kenneth."

"My secretary said...." The Mayor sounded angry now, although he knew Ken well.

"I didn't say my father was calling," said Ken. "I've got something to say that I think you will want to hear, and it will take only a minute."

"All right. Go ahead."

"In a day or two the entire town is going to be without power, transportation, or communication with the outside world. The science club of the high school has a 1000-watt amateur transmitter that can reach any point in the United States and most foreign countries. It requires power. We can operate from batteries, and I would like to ask you to authorize that all automobile batteries and those belonging to the telephone company be immediately seized by the city and placed in official custody, to be used for emergency communication purposes only. They should be drained of electrolyte and properly stored."

"I appreciate that suggestion," the Mayor said. "I think it's a good one. Would you boys be able to take care of that?"

"We'd be glad to."

"It's your assignment, then. We are calling a town meeting tonight in the college auditorium. We especially want your father to be there if he can, and we'll issue orders for the battery conservation program at that time."

By noon Ken had gained an interview with President Lewis and had received permission for his group to make use of the largest blower on the campus for their air-sampling project. They loaded their tools and themselves into the ancient wagon belonging to Dave Whitaker's uncle and spent the rest of the day working at Science Hall.

Ken's father called again to report they had succeeded in renting a horse and buggy at an exorbitant price from a farmer. When told of the town meeting that evening, he promised to try to reach Mayfield in time.

Ten minutes before the 8 o'clock deadline, Professor Maddox drew up in front of the house. He called to Ken without even getting down from the seat of the wagon. "Get your mother, and let's go!"

Mrs. Maddox appeared, worried and concerned. "You've had nothing to eat," she protested. "At least come in and have a sandwich and a glass of milk. It's not cold, but it's fresh."

"No." Professor Maddox shook his head. "We don't want to miss any of the meeting. Get a coat and come along. It will be chilly later."

Maria and her mother came also. The small wagon was loaded to capacity as it moved slowly up the hill toward the campus. People were streaming toward the auditorium from all directions. Most of them were afoot. A few others had found a horse and wagon. A dozen or two cars chugged protestingly up the hill, but it appeared that most of these would not be operating another 24 hours.

As they approached the hall, Professor Maddox chuckled and pointed a finger ahead of them. "Look there. I'm sure that every citizen of Mayfield is present or accounted for, now."

Ken glanced in the direction of his father's gesture. The creaky wagon of Granny Wicks was drawn slowly along by her emaciated horse. Granny's stick-thin body jounced harshly on the rough seat. Ken fought against a ridiculous uneasiness as he recognized her.

He knew his father had not heard Granny's speech on the post office steps, but he was little surprised when his father said, "I'm afraid Granny Wicks, with her profound knowledge of omens and signs, is about as much an authority on this matter as any of the rest of us here tonight!"

5
THIEF

The hall was already filled. Several scores of chairs had been placed in the corridors, and these were occupied also. People were being ushered to nearby classrooms where they would hear the proceedings over the school's public-address system.

"It looks as if we'll have to get it by remote pickup," said Ken. At that moment Sally Teasdale, the Mayor's secretary, spotted their group and hurried over.

"Mayor Hilliard told me to watch for you," she said. "He wants you to sit on the platform, Professor Maddox, and also Dr. Douglas and Dr. Larsen. The others of your party can sit in the wings."

Professor Maddox agreed and they followed Sally to the stage entrance. The platform was already occupied by the Mayor and the town councilmen, the college department heads, and leading citizens of Mayfield. The professors took their places, while Ken and the others found chairs in the wings. It was the best seat in the house, Ken decided. They could see both the platform and the audience below.

It was undoubtedly the largest group that had ever gathered in one place in Mayfield. In spite of the enormous number present it was a solemn group. There was almost no talking or jostling. To Ken, it seemed the faces about him had a uniform appearance of bewildered searching for reassurance that nothing could really destroy the way of life they had always known.

Mayor Hilliard arose and called the meeting to order. "I think everyone knows why we've been called here," he said. "Because of the nature of the circumstances I think it appropriate that we ask Dr. Aylesworth, pastor of the Community Church, to offer prayer."

Heads were bowed in reverent silence as Dr. Aylesworth stood before the assembly and offered a solemn invocation that their deliberations might receive divine guidance, and their minds be filled with wisdom to combat the evil that had come upon them.

The minister was a big, ruddy-faced man with a lion's mane of white hair. The unwavering authority of his voice filled the audience with the conviction that they were better prepared to face their problems when he had resumed his seat.

Mayor Hilliard outlined the worldwide situation as he had obtained it through news reports up to an hour ago. He described the desperate situation of the nation's larger cities. Their food supplies were sufficient for only a few days without any replenishment by rail and truck transportation. Ninety percent of automobile traffic had ceased. The railroads were attempting to conserve their rolling stock, but 70 percent of it was out of commission, and the remainder could not be expected to operate longer than a few days. Air traffic had stopped entirely. On the oceans, only sailing vessels continued to move.

"Mayfield is already cut off," the Mayor went on. "Our last train went through here 30 hours ago. The trucking companies out of Frederick have suspended operations. We have no cars or trucks of our own here in town, on which we can depend. We're on our own.

"So far, the scientists have found no solution. Tomorrow, they may find one. Or it may be 10 years before they do. In the meantime, we have to figure out how we, here in Mayfield, are going to carry on.

"Our first consideration is, of course, food supplies. The Council met this morning, and we have appointed a committee to take immediate possession of all foodstuffs and every facility for food production within the entire valley. Beginning tomorrow morning, this committee will begin to accumulate all food supplies into one or more central warehouses where they will be inventoried for rationing.

"All stocks of fresh meat will be salted and cured. Home supplies will be limited to no more than a week's needs of any one item. Hoarders who persist in their unfair activities will be ordered to leave the community.

"My fellow citizens, these are stringent and severe regulations, but we are not facing a time of mild inconvenience. It may well be that in this coming winter we shall be literally fighting for our very lives. We, as your leaders, would like a vote of confidence from you, the citizens of Mayfield, as an assurance that you will co-operate with our efforts to the best of your ability."

Instantly, nearly everyone in the auditorium was on his feet shouting his approval of the Mayor's program.

Mayor Hilliard had known he was taking a long chance in presenting so bluntly such a severe program, but long experience had taught him the best way into a tough situation was a headlong plunge that ignored consequences. The ovation surprised him. He had expected substantial opposition. Visibly moved, he held up his hand for quiet once more.

"Our farms and our livestock will be our only means of salvation after present food stocks are gone," he said. "A separate subcommittee will inventory all farmland and cattle and dairy herds and plan for their most efficient use in the coming season. Crops will be assigned as the committee sees fit. Farm labor will be taken care of by all of us, on a community basis.

"A third program that must begin immediately is the stockpiling of fuel for the coming winter. Wood will be our only means of heating and cooking because the nearest mines are too far away for us to haul coal from them by teams. The same is true of fuel oil stocks.

"Heating will be at a minimum. Most of you do not have wood stoves. What you have must be converted to use of wood. An additional committee will be appointed to supervise this conversion and the construction, where necessary, of makeshift stoves out of sheet metal, old oil barrels, and anything else of which we can make use."

Item by item, he continued down the list of problems the Council had considered that day. He mentioned Ken's suggestion for conservation of batteries. He spoke of the problems of medical care without adequate hospital facilities, of police activities that might be required in a period of stress such as they could expect that winter.

When he had finished, members of the Council detailed plans of the separate programs over which they had charge. President Lewis spoke to pledge support of the college staff. He pointed out the fortunate fact that they had some of the best minds in the entire country in their scientific departments, and also had Professor Larsen visiting with them.

The floor was turned over then to members of the audience for comment and questions. Most of them were favorable, but Sam Cluff, who owned a hundred and sixty of the best acres in the valley, stood up red-faced and belligerent.

"It's all a pack of nonsense!" he declared. "This is just an excuse for certain people in this town to get their hands in somebody else's pockets, and to tell other people what to do and how to live.

"I'm not going to have anything to do with it. Anybody who sets foot on my land to tell me what to raise or to take my goods away is going to have to reckon with a double-barreled, 12-gauge shotgun.

"If there is any real problem, which I doubt, them Government scientists will be on the job and get things straightened out so that trains and automobiles will be running by next week. My advice is for everybody to go home and let them take care of it."

Mayor Hilliard smiled tolerantly. "I shouldn't have to remind you, Sam, that some of the best scientists in the world are right here in our own town, and they say the situation is serious enough for emergency measures. I hope you won't be foolish with that shotgun, but we're coming out to see you, tomorrow, Sam."

Granny Wicks seemed to erupt from her place to which she had crowded in the center of the hall. All eyes turned at the sound of her scratchy, birdlike voice. "I told you," she shrieked. "I told you what was coming, and now maybe you'll believe me. There's nothing you can do about it, Bill Hilliard. Nothing at all. There's death in the air. The stars have spoken it. The signs are in the sky."

Mayor Hilliard interrupted her. "Perhaps you're right, Granny," he said gently. "I don't think any of us are going to argue with you tonight. We're here to do what we can, and to make plans to stay alive just as long as possible."

At the close, Dr. Aylesworth took the stand. His commanding presence seemed to draw an aura of peace once more around the troubled group. "We are civilized men and women," he said. "Let us see that we act as such during the months that are ahead of us. Let us remember that we may see a time very soon when there will not be enough food, fuel and clothing for all of us. When and if that time comes, let us prove that we are able to be our brother's keeper, that we are able to do unto others as we would have others do unto us. Above all, may we be able to continue to call on divine assistance to bring a speedy end to this disaster, so that when it is over we can look back and be proud that we conducted ourselves as men and women worthy to be called civilized, and worthy of the divine approval and aid which we now seek."

It was decided to keep classes going in the various schools as long as possible, releasing those students who were needed to take assignments in the emergency program. Ken and the rest of the science club members obtained immediate permission to devote their full time to the research program.

On the morning after the town meeting, Ken dressed early and rode his bicycle toward Art's garage to arrange with the mechanic the details of the gathering and

storage of automobile batteries. On the way he passed by
Frank Meggs Independent Grocery Market, the largest in
Mayfield.

Although it was only a little after 7 o'clock, an
enormous crowd had collected outside and inside the
store. Curious and half-alarmed, Ken parked his bicycle
and made his way through the crowd. Inside, he found
Frank Meggs ringing up sales of large lots of food.

A red-faced woman was arguing with him at the
check-out stand. "A dollar a pound for white beans! That's
ridiculous, Frank Meggs, and you know it!"

"Sure I know it," the storekeeper said calmly. "Next
winter you'll be glad I let you have them for even that
price. If you don't want them, Mrs. Watkins, please move
along. Others will be glad to have them."

The woman hesitated, then angrily flung two bills on
the counter and stalked out with her groceries. Ken
shoved his way up to the stand. "Mr. Meggs," he
exclaimed. "You can't do this! All foodstuffs are being
called in by the Mayor's committee."

He turned to the people. "Private hoards of food will
be confiscated and placed in the community warehouse.
This isn't going to do you any good!"

Most of the shoppers looked shamefaced, at his
challenge, but Meggs bristled angrily. "You keep out of
this, Maddox! Nobody asked you to come in here! These
people know what they're doing, and so do I. How much
do you think any of us will eat if townhall gets its hands
on every scrap of food in the valley? If you aren't buying,
get moving!"

"I will, and I'll be back just as soon as I can find the
Sheriff!"

With telephone service now cut off to conserve battery
power, Ken hesitated between seeking Sheriff Johnson at
his office or at home. He checked his watch again and
decided on the Sheriff's home.

He was fortunate in arriving just before the Sheriff
left. He explained quickly what was happening at Meggs'

store. Johnson had been assigned one of the few
remaining cars that would run. With Ken, he drove
immediately to the store. They strode in, the shoppers
fanning out before the Sheriff's approach.

"Okay, that's all," he said. "You folks leave your
groceries right where they are. Tell the others they had
better bring theirs back and get their money while Meggs
still has it. Not that anybody is going to have much use
for money, anyway."

"You've no right to do this!" Meggs cried. "This is my
private property and I'm entitled to do with it as I
choose!"

"Not any longer it isn't," said Sheriff Johnson. "There
isn't such a thing as private property in Mayfield, any
more. Except maybe the shirt on your back, and I'm not
sure of that. At any rate, you're not selling these
groceries. Accounts will be kept, and when and if we get
back to normal you'll be reimbursed, but for now we're all
one, big, happy family!"

Most of the crowd had dispersed. The armloads and
pushcarts full of groceries had been abandoned. Ken and
the Sheriff moved toward the door.

"Another trick like that and you'll spend the time of
the emergency as a guest of the city. Incidentally, we
don't intend to heat the jail this winter!"

Meggs turned the blaze of his anger upon Ken. "This
is your fault!" he snarled. "You and that bunch of
politicians know there's not going to be any shortage this
winter just as well as I do. In a week this whole thing will
be straightened out. I had a chance to make a good thing
of it. I'm going to get even with you if it's the last thing I
ever do!"

"That's enough of that!" said Sheriff Johnson sharply.
"Come along, Ken."

Ken was not disturbed by Meggs' threat of personal
retaliation, but he was frightened by the realization that
Meggs wasn't the only one of his kind in Mayfield. His

patrons were only a shade less unstable. What would such people do when things really got tough? How much could they be depended on to pull their own weight?

After he had seen Art Matthews about collecting and storing the batteries, Ken went up to Science Hall where the rest of the club members were already at work. Under the direction of Al Miner, who was the best qualified to plan the alterations of the ventilation ducts, they made the necessary changes and installed one of the motorcycle engines to drive the blower. At the same time, three of them built up a high-voltage, battery-operated power supply to charge the filter elements.

By evening the assembly was operating. The motorcycle engine chugged pleasantly. "I wonder how long before that one freezes up," Al said pessimistically.

"We ought to get more," said Joe. "The way the cars have gone we'll be lucky to get more than 2 days out of each one of these."

During the day, Ken's father had directed the preparation of metallic specimens from samples the boys had brought from Art's garage and from those the men brought back from the power plant. With the high-powered electron microscope, photographs were taken.

As they finished their work the boys went with Ken to the laboratory. Professor Maddox looked up. "Hello, Fellows," he said. "Have you got your piece of machinery running?"

"Purring like a top," said Ken.

"Expected to run about as long," said Al.

"Have you finished any photomicrographs?" Ken asked. "Do they show anything?"

His father passed over a wet print. The boys gathered around it.

"It doesn't mean much to me," said Dave Whitaker. "Can you tell us what it shows?"

Ken's father took a pencil from his pocket and touched it lightly to a barely perceptible line across the center of the picture. "That is the boundary," he said, "between the cylinder wall and the piston taken from one of the samples you brought in."

"I can't see anything that looks like a line between two pieces of metal," said Ted Watkins. "It looks like one solid chunk to me."

"That is substantially what it is," said Professor Maddox. "There is no longer any real boundary as there would be between two ordinary pieces of metal. Molecules from each piece have flowed into the other, mixing just as two very viscous liquids would do. They have actually become one piece of metal."

He took up another photograph. "Here you can see that the same thing has happened in the case of the shaft and bearing samples we obtained from the Collin's Dam power plant. Molecules of the two separate pieces of metal have intermingled, becoming one single piece."

"How could they do that?" Ken exclaimed. "Metals can't flow like liquids."

"They can if the conditions are right. When steel is heated to a sufficiently high temperature, it flows like water."

"But that's not the case here!"

"No, it isn't, of course. At lower temperatures the molecules of a solid do not possess the energy of motion which they have in a liquid state. The metallic surface of a piece of cold steel has a certain surface tension which prevents the escape of the relatively low-energy molecules; thus it has the characteristics we ascribe to a solid."

"Then what has happened in this case?" Joe asked. "Are you able to tell?"

Professor Maddox nodded. "The photographs show us what has happened, but they reveal nothing about how or why. We can see the surface tension of the two pieces of metal has obviously broken down so that the small energy of motion possessed by the molecules has permitted them to move toward each other, with a consequent mixing of the two metals. It has turned them quite literally into a single piece, the most effective kind of weld you can imagine."

"What would cause the surface tension to break down like that?" Ken asked.

"That is what remains for us to find out. We don't have the faintest idea what has caused it. It becomes especially baffling when we recall that it has happened, not in a single isolated instance, but all over the world."

"You would think the metals would have become soft, like putty, or something, for a thing like that to happen to them," said Joe.

"It would be expected that the hardness would be affected. This is not true, however. The metals seem just as hard as before. The effect of mixing seems to take place only when the metals are in sliding motion against one another, as in the case of a piston and cylinder, or a shaft and a bearing. The effect is comparatively slow, taking place over a number of days. The two surfaces must break down gradually, increasing the friction to a point where motion must cease. Then the mixing continues until they are welded solidly to each other."

Ordinarily, the dusk of evening would have fallen over the landscape, but the blaze of the comet now lit the countryside with an unnatural gold that reflected like a flame through the windows and onto the faces of the men and boys in the laboratory.

"As to the cause of this phenomenon," Professor Maddox said with an obviously weary deliberation in his voice, "we can only hope to find an explanation and a cure before it is too late to do the world any good."

"There can't be any question of that!" said Ken intensely. "The resources of the whole scientific world will be turned on this one problem. Every industrial, university, and governmental laboratory will be working on it. Modern science can certainly lick a thing like this!"

Professor Maddox turned from the window, which he had been facing. A faint, grim smile touched the corners of his lips and died as he regarded the boys, especially Ken. His face took on a depth of soberness Ken seldom saw in his father.

"You think nothing is immune to an attack by so-called modern science?" he said.

"Sure!" Ken went on enthusiastically, not understanding the expression on his father's face. "Look at the problems that have been licked as soon as people were determined enough and willing to pay the cost. Giant computers, radar eyes, atomic energy. Everybody knows we could have made it to Mars by now if governments had been willing to put up the necessary money."

"You still have to learn, all of you do," Professor Maddox said slowly, "that the thing we call science is only a myth. The only reality consists of human beings trying to solve difficult problems. Their results, which seem to be solutions to some of those problems, we call science. Science has no life of its own. It does not deserve to be spoken of as an entity in its own right. There are only people, whom we call scientists, and their accomplishments are severely limited by their quite meager abilities. Meager, when viewed in comparison with the magnitude of the problems they attack."

Ken felt bewildered. He had never heard his father speak this way before. "Don't you believe there are scientists enough–scientists who know enough–to lick a thing like this in time?"

"I don't know. I'm quite sure no one knows. We became conscious long ago of the fallacy of assuming that the concentration of men enough and unlimited funds would solve any problem in the world. For every great accomplishment like atomic energy, to which we point with pride, there are a thousand other problems, equally important, that remain unsolved. Who knows whether or not this problem of weakened surface tension in metals is one of the insoluble ones?"

"We have to find an answer," said Ken doggedly. He could not understand his father's words. "There's nothing science can't accomplish if it sets about it with enough determination. Nothing!"

6
THE SCIENTIST

Ken spent an almost sleepless night. He tossed for long hours and dozed finally, but he awoke again before there was even a trace of dawn in the sky. Although the night was cool he was sweating as if it were mid-summer.

There was a queasiness in his stomach, too, a slow undefinable pressure on some hidden nerve he had never known he possessed. The feeling pulsed and throbbed slowly and painfully. He sat up and looked out at the dark landscape, and he knew what was the matter.

Scared, he thought, I'm scared sick.

He'd never known anything like it before in his life, except maybe the time when he was 6 years old and he had climbed to the top of a very high tree when the wind was blowing, and he had been afraid to come down.

It was hitting him, he thought. He was just beginning to understand what this stoppage of machinery really meant, and he wondered if there was something wrong with him that he had not felt it earlier. Was he alone? Had everyone else understood it before he had? Or would it hit them, one by one, just as it was hitting him now, bringing him face to face with what lay ahead.

He knew what had done it. It was his father's expression and his words in the laboratory the night before.

Ken recognized that he had never doubted for an instant that scientists and their tools were wholly adequate to solve this problem in a reasonable time. He had been aware there would be great hardships, but he had never doubted there would be an end to that time. He had believed his father, as a scientist, had the same faith.

It was a staggering shock to learn that his father had no faith in science; a shock to be told that science was not a thing that warranted a man's faith. Ken had planned his whole life around an avid faith in science.

He tried to imagine what the world would be like if no engine should ever run again. The standards of civilized existence would be shattered. Only those areas of the world, where people had never learned to depend on motor transportation or electric power, would be unaffected; those areas of China, India and Africa, where men still scratched the ground with a forked stick and asked only for a cup of rice or grain each day.

This would become the level of the whole world. Until last night, Ken had never believed it remotely possible. Now, his father's words had shaken him out of the certainty that science would avert such consequences. It *could* happen.

He thought of his own plans and ambitions. There would be no need for scientists, nor the opportunity to become one, in a world of men who grubbed the land with forked sticks. He felt a sudden blind and bitter anger. Even if the disaster were overcome in a matter of years, his opportunity would be gone.

He knew at once that such anger was selfish and futile. His own personal calamities would be the least of the troubles ahead, but, for the moment, he could not help it. In a way, it felt good because it overshadowed the dark fear that still throbbed in his body.

But something else was gone, too. The opportunity for him and his science club friends to investigate the properties of the altered metal was over. His father and the other scientists had taken over those studies, and there would be no place for high-school boys who did not know even enough to prepare a slide for an electron microscope.

It had always been that way, as long as he could remember. He had always been too young and too ignorant to be intrusted with work that mattered.

He supposed they would turn the operation of the air filter over to one of the teaching fellows, even though that was something the club could handle.

The bitterness and the fear seemed more than he could endure. He dressed quietly and went downstairs. Without lighting a lamp, he found something to eat. The first light of dawn was showing when he left the house.

For an hour he walked the silent streets without meeting anyone. Normally, there would have been the sound of milk trucks, and the cars of early-rising workers. Now there was nothing. The comet had risen just above the eastern hills, and in its light the city was like some fabulous, golden ruin that belonged in an ancient fairytale.

Ken didn't know where he was going or what he was going to do. There ought to be something useful he could do, he thought fiercely.

As he looked down the street, he saw a half-dozen wagons with two teams each, stopped in front of Sims Hardware and Lumber. In the wagons were several dozen men. Ken recognized Andrew Norton, of the Mayor's Council, and Henry Atkins, the Sheriff's chief deputy.

Several of the men were emerging from the hardware store with new axes and saws. Then Ken understood. This was the first wood detail headed for the mountains to begin gathering and stockpiling fuel for the winter. He broke into a run.

Deputy Atkins appeared to be in charge of the group. Ken hailed him. "I want to go along, Mr. Atkins. May I go?"

The deputy glanced down at him and frowned. He consulted a sheet of paper he drew from his pocket. "Your name isn't on the list for this morning, Ken. Were you assigned?"

"I guess not, but I haven't got anything else to do today. Is there any objection to my going?"

"I don't suppose so," said Atkins dubiously. "It's just that your name may be on some other list. We don't want to get these things fouled up right off the bat. There's enough trouble as it is."

"I'm sure my name's not on any other list. I'd have been told about it."

"All right. Climb on."

As Ken climbed into the nearest wagon he was startled to find himself staring into the face of Frank Meggs. The storekeeper grinned unpleasantly as he nodded his head in Ken's direction and spoke to his neighbor. "Now what do you know about that? Old Man Maddox, letting his own little boy out alone this early in the morning. I'll bet he didn't let you, did he? I'll bet you had to run away to try to prove you're a big boy now."

"Cut it out, Meggs," said Atkins sharply. "We heard all about what went on in your store yesterday."

The man next to Meggs drew away, but it didn't seem to bother him. He continued to grin crookedly at Ken. "Aren't you afraid you might get hurt trying to do a man's work?"

Ken ignored the jibes and faced away from the storekeeper. The slow, rhythmic jogging of the wagon, and the frosty air as they came into the mountains took some of the bitterness out of Ken. It made him feel freshly alive. He had come often to hunt here and felt a familiarity with every tree and rock around him.

The wagon train came to a halt in a grove of 10-year-old saplings that needed thinning.

"No use taking our best timber until we have to," said Atkins. "We'll start here. I'll take a crew and go on ahead and mark the ones to be cut. You drivers unhitch your teams and drag the logs out to the wagons after they're cut."

There was none of the kidding and horseplay that would have been normal in such a group. Each man seemed intent on the purpose for which he had come, and was absorbed with his own thoughts. Ken took a double-bitted ax and followed Atkins along the trail. He moved away from the others and began cutting one of the young trees Atkins had marked.

By noon he was bathed in sweat, and his arms and back ached. He had thought he was in good condition from his football and track work, but he seemed to have found new muscles that had never come into play before.

Atkins noticed the amount he had cut and complimented him. "Better take it easy. You're way ahead of everybody else, and we don't have to get it all out today."

Ken grinned, enjoying the aches of his muscles. "If it has to be done we might as well do it."

He was not surprised to find that Frank Meggs had cut almost nothing but had spent his time complaining to his companions about the unnecessary work they were doing.

After lunch, which Ken had reluctantly accepted from the others, there was a stir at the arrival of a newcomer on horseback. Ken recognized him as Mike Travis, one of the carpenters and caretakers at the college.

Mike tied his horse to the tailboard of a wagon and approached the woodcutters. "There you are, Ken Maddox," he said accusingly. "Why didn't you let somebody know where you were going? Your father's been chewing up everyone in sight, trying to find out where you'd gone. He finally decided you might be up here, and sent me after you. Take the horse on back. I'll finish up the day on the wood detail."

Ken felt suddenly awkward and uncomfortable. "I didn't mean to worry him, but I guess I did forget to say where I was going. Don't you think it would be okay if I stayed and you told Dad you had found me?"

"Not on your life! He'd chew me down to the ankles if I went back without you!"

"Okay, I'll go," Ken said. Although he knew he should have left word it still seemed strange that his father should be so concerned as to send a man up here looking for him. It seemed like more of the unfamiliar facets of his father's personality that Ken had glimpsed last night.

Frank Meggs was watching from across the clearing. "I guess Papa Maddox couldn't stand the thought of his little boy doing a man's work for a whole day," he said loudly and maliciously. No one paid any attention to him.

*   *   *   *   *

Ken tied the mare to a tree on the campus where she could graze. He glanced over the valley below. Not a single car was in sight on the roads. Somehow, it was beginning to seem that this was the way it had always been. His own car seemed like something he had possessed a thousand years ago.

He found his father in the laboratory working with the electron microscope. Professor Maddox looked up and gestured toward the office. As Ken sat down, he shut the door behind them and took a seat behind his old oak desk that was still cluttered with unmarked examination papers.

"You didn't say anything about where you were going this morning," he said.

"I'm sorry about that," Ken answered. "I got up early and took a walk through town. All of a sudden—well, I guess I got panicky when it finally hit me as to what all this really means. I saw the wood detail going out and joined them. It felt good out there, with nothing to think about except getting a tree to fall right."

"You ran away. You were needed here."

Ken stammered. "I didn't think you wanted any of us kids around since you and the other men had taken over what we had started to do."

"You were angry that it wasn't your own show any longer, weren't you?"

"I guess that's part of it," Ken admitted, his face reddening. He didn't know what was happening. His father had never spoken to him like this before. He seemed suddenly critical and disapproving of everything about Ken.

After a long time his father spoke again, more gently this time. "It's been your ambition for a long time to be a scientist, hasn't it?"

"You know it has."

"I've been very pleased, too. I've watched you and encouraged your interests and, as far as I can see, you've been developing in the right direction."

"I'm glad you think so," Ken said.

"But you've wanted to be a *great* scientist. You've had an ambition to emulate men like Newton, Faraday, Davy, and the modern giants such as Einstein, Planck, de Broglie, Oppenheimer."

"Maybe I haven't got the brains, but I can try."

His father snorted impatiently. "Do you think any one of them tried deliberately to be great, or to copy anyone else?"

Ken understood his meaning now. "I guess they didn't. You can't really do a thing like that."

"No, you can't. You take the brains God has given you and apply them to the universe as you see it. The results take care of themselves.

"Some of us have enough insight to achieve greatness. Most of us lack the cleverness to cope effectively with such a wily opponent as the natural universe. Greatness and mediocrity have no meaning to a man who is absorbed in his study. You do what you have to do. You do what the best and highest impulses of your brain tell you to do. Expect nothing more than this of yourself. Nothing more is possible."

"I think I see what you mean," Ken said.

"I doubt it. Most of the men I know have never learned it. They struggle to write more papers, to get their names in more journals than their colleagues. They go out of their way to be patted on the back.

"They are the failures as scientists. For an example of success I recommend that you observe Dr. Larsen closely. He is a man who has done a great deal to advance our knowledge of physical chemistry."

Professor Maddox paused. Then he said finally, "There is just one other thing."

"What's that?" Ken asked.

"Up to now, you and all your friends have only played at science."

"Played!" Ken cried. "We've built our observatory, a 1000-watt radio transmitter–"

"Play; these things are toys. Educational toys, it is true, but toys, nevertheless."

"I don't understand."

"Toys are fine for children. You and your friends, however, are no longer children. You haven't got a chance now to grow up and gain an education in a normal manner. You can't finish your childhood, playing with your toys. You can't take all the time you need to find out what your capacities and aptitudes are. You will never know a world that will allow you that luxury.

"Every available brain is needed on this problem. You've got to make a decision today, this very minute, whether you want to give a hand to its solution."

"You know I want to be in on it!"

"Do you? Then you've got to decide that you are no longer concerned about being a scientist. Forget the word. What you are does not matter. You are simply a man with a problem to solve.

"You have to decide whether or not you can abandon your compassion for the millions who are going to die; whether you can reject all pressure from personal danger, and from the threat to everything and everyone that is of any importance to you.

"You've got to decide whether or not this problem of the destruction of surface tension of metals is the most absorbing thing in the whole world. It needs solving, not because the fate of the world hinges on it, but because it's a problem that consumes you utterly. This is what drives you, not fear, not danger, not the opinion of anyone else.

"When he can function this way, the scientist is capable of solving important problems. By outward heartlessness he can achieve works of compassion greater than any of his critics. He knows that the greatest pleasure a man can know lies in taking a stand against those forces that bend ordinary men."

For the first time in his life Ken suddenly felt that he knew his father. "I wish you had talked to me like this a long time ago," he said.

Professor Maddox shook his head. "It would have been far better for you to find out these things for yourself. My telling you does not convince you they are true. That conviction must still come from within."

"Do you want me to become a scientist?" Ken asked.

"It doesn't make any difference what I want," his father answered almost roughly. He was looking away from Ken and then his eyes found his son's and his glance softened. He reached across the desk and grasped Ken's hand.

"Yes, I want it more than anything else in the world," he said earnestly. "But it's got to be what you want, too, or it's no good at all. Don't try to be anything for my sake. Determine your own goals clearly, and take as straight a path as you can to reach them. Just remember, if you do choose science the standards are severe."

"It's what I want," said Ken evenly. "You said you needed me here. What do you want me to do?"

"Empty trash cans if we ask it," Professor Maddox said. "Forget about whose show it is. Professor Larsen and I will be directing the research, and we'll need every pair of hands and every brain that's got an ounce of intelligence in this field. You do whatever you are asked to do and think of every possible answer to the questions that come before you. Is that good enough?"

"More than enough." Ken felt a sudden stinging sensation behind his eyes and turned to rub their corners roughly. "What about the other fellows in the club? Can you use them, too?"

"As many as have the ounce of intelligence I spoke of. The rest of them don't need to know the things I have told you, but with you it was different. I had to know you understood just a little of what it means to be a scientist."

"I'll be one. I'll show you I can be one!"

7
DUST FROM THE STARS

Ken felt he had grown 3 inches taller after his father's discussion. As if he had passed some ancient ritual, he could be admitted to the company of adults and his opinions would be heard.

This proved to be true. His father rapidly organized the facilities of the college laboratories and recruited every possible science student in the chemistry and physics departments, as well as many from the high school. As these plans were outlined, Ken made a proposal of his own.

"I believe our first move," he said, "should be to set up a network of amateur radio stations operating in cities where there are other laboratories. If you could be in touch with them, ideas could be exchanged and duplication of work avoided."

"An excellent idea," said Professor Maddox. "You can work it out as we go along."

"No. It ought to be done immediately," Ken said. "If not, it may be almost impossible to find anyone on the air later. There may not be many amateurs who will bother to convert their rigs to battery operation. There may not be many who can get the batteries together."

"Good enough!" his father said. "Let that have priority over everything else until you get it organized. Probably you should find at least two contacts in each of the university centers. Put at the top of your list Berkeley, Pasadena, Chicago, New York, and Washington, D.C.

"See if you can get relay contacts that will put us in touch with Stockholm, Paris, London, Berlin, and Tokyo.

If so, we can have contact with the majority of the
workers capable of contributing most to this problem."

"I'll do my best," Ken promised.

Someone would be needed to operate the station and
spend a good many hours a week listening and recording.
He didn't want to spend the time necessary doing that,
and he knew none of the other club members would,
either. At once he thought of Maria Larsen. She would
undoubtedly be happy to take over the job and feel she
was doing something useful. On the way home he stopped
at her house and told her what he had in mind. She
readily agreed.

"I don't know anything about radio," she said. "You'll
have to show me what to do."

"We won't expect you to learn code, of course," he said.
"When we do handle anything coming in by code one of us
will have to take it. We'll try to contact phone stations
wherever possible for this program we have in mind.
Most of the stuff will be put on tape, and Dad will
probably want you to prepare typed copies, too. You can
do enough to take a big load off the rest of us."

"I'll be happy to try."

They spent the rest of the day in the radio room of the
science shack. Ken taught Maria the simple operations of
turning on the transmitter and receiver, of handling the
tuning controls, and the proper procedure for making and
receiving calls. He supposed there would be some
technical objection to her operation of the station without
an operator's license, but he was quite sure that such
things were not important right now.

It was a new kind of experience for Maria. Her face
was alive with excitement as Ken checked several bands
to see where amateurs were still operating. The babble of
high-frequency code whistles alternated in the room with
faint, sometimes muffled voices on the phone band.

"There are more stations than I expected," Ken said.
"With luck, we may be able to establish a few of the
contacts we need, tonight."

After many tries, he succeeded in raising an operator, W6YRE, in San Francisco. They traded news, and it sounded as if the west coast city was crumbling swiftly. Ken explained what he wanted. W6YRE promised to try to raise someone with a high-powered phone rig in Berkeley, near the university.

They listened to him calling, but could not hear the station he finally raised.

"What good will that do?" Maria asked. "If we can't hear the station in Berkeley...."

"He may be working on a relay deal through the small rig. It's better than nothing, but I'd prefer a station we can contact directly."

In a few minutes, the San Francisco operator called them back. "W6WGU knows a ham with a 1000-watt phone near the university," he said. "He thinks he'll go for your deal, but he's not set up for battery. In fact, he's about ready to evacuate. Maybe he can be persuaded to stay. I'm told he's a guy who will do the noble thing if he sees a reason for it."

"There's plenty of reason for this," said Ken.

"Let's set a schedule for 9 p.m. I ought to have word on it by then."

They agreed and cut off. In another hour they had managed a contact with a Chicago operator, and explained what they wanted.

"You're out of luck here," the ham replied. "This town is falling apart at the seams right now. The whole Loop area has been burned out. There's been rioting for 18 hours straight. The militia have been trying to hold things together, but I don't think they even know whether anybody is still on top giving the orders.

"I'll try to find out what the eggheads at the university are doing, but if they've got any kind of research running in this mess, it'll surprise me. If they are still there, I'll hang on and report to you. Otherwise, I'm heading north. There's not much sense to it, but when something like this happens a guy's got to run or have a good reason for staying put. If he doesn't he'll go nuts."

The Chicago operator agreed to a schedule for the following morning.

Maria and Ken sat in silence, not looking at each other, after they cut off.

"It will be that way in all the big cities, won't it?" Maria asked.

"I'm afraid so. We're luckier than they are," Ken said, "but I wonder how long we'll stay lucky." He was thinking of Frank Meggs, and the people who had swamped his store.

At 9 p.m., W6YRE came back on. The Berkeley 1000-watt phone was enthusiastic about being a contact post with the university people. He had promised to make arrangements with them and to round up enough batteries to convert his transmitter and receiver.

They had no further success that night.

Ken's father shook his head sadly when told of the situation in Chicago. "I had counted on them," he said. "Their people are among the best in the world, and they have the finest equipment. I hope things are not like that everywhere."

Members of the science club took turns at the transmitter the following days for 20-hour stretches, until everything possible had been done to establish the contacts requested by Professor Maddox.

In Chicago there appeared to have been a complete collapse. The operator there reported he was unable to reach any of the scientific personnel at the university. He promised a further contact, but when the time came he could not be reached. There was no voice at all in the Chicago area. Ken wondered what had become of the man whose voice they had heard briefly. He was certain he would never know.

Although there was much disorder on the west coast, the situation was in somewhat better control. The rioting had not yet threatened the universities, and both

Berkeley and Pasadena were working frantically on the problem with round-the-clock shifts in their laboratories. They had welcomed wholeheartedly the communication network initiated by the Mayfield group.

In Washington, D.C. tight military control was keeping things somewhat in order. In Stockholm, where contact had been established through a Washington relay after 2 days of steady effort, there was no rioting whatever. Paris and London had suffered, but their leading universities were at work on the problem. Tokyo reported similar conditions.

Ken grinned at Maria as they received the Stockholm report. "Those Swedes," he said. "They're pretty good at keeping their heads."

Maria answered with a faint smile of her own. "Everybody should be Swedes. No?"

*   *   *   *   *

The fall winds and the black frost came early that year, as if in fair warning that the winter intended a brutal assault upon the stricken world. The pile of logs in the community woodlot grew steadily. A large crew of men worked to reduce the logs to stove lengths.

They had made a crude attempt to set up a circular saw, using animal power to drive it. The shaft was mounted in hardwood blocks, driven by a complicated arrangement of wooden pulleys and leather belts. The horses worked it through a treadmill.

The apparatus worked part of the time, but it scarcely paid for itself when measured against the efforts of the men who had to keep it in repair.

The food storage program was well underway. Two central warehouses had been prepared from the converted Empire Movie Theater, and the Rainbow Skating Rink.

Ken wished their efforts at the college laboratory were going half as well. As the days passed, it seemed they were getting nowhere. The first effort to identify any foreign substance in the atmospheric dust was a failure. Calculations showed they had probably not allowed sufficient time to sample a large enough volume of air.

It was getting increasingly difficult to keep the blower system going. All of their original supply of small engines had broken down. The town had been scoured for replacements. These, too, were failing.

In the metallurgical department hundreds of tests had been run on samples taken from frozen engines. The photomicrographs all showed a uniform peculiarity, which the scientists could not explain. Embedded in the crystalline structure of the metal were what appeared to be some kind of foreign, amorphous particles which were concentrated near the line of union of the two parts.

Berkeley and Pasadena confirmed these results with their own tests. There was almost unanimous belief that it was in no way connected with the comet. Ken stood almost alone in his dogged conviction that the Earth's presence in the tail of the comet could be responsible for the catastrophe.

Another theory that was gaining increasing acceptance was that this foreign substance was an unexpected by-product of the hydrogen and atomic bomb testing that had been going on for so many years. Ken was forced to admit the possibility of this, inasmuch as radiation products were scattered heavily now throughout the Earth's atmosphere. Both Russia and Britain had conducted extensive tests just before the breakdowns began occurring.

The members of the science club had been allowed to retain complete control of the air-sampling program. They washed the filters carefully at intervals and distilled the solvent to recover the precious residue of dust.

As the small quantity of this grew after another week of collecting, it was treated to remove the ordinary carbon particles and accumulated pollens. When this was done there was very little remaining, but that little something might be ordinary dust carried into the atmosphere from the surface of the Earth. Or it might be out of the tail of the comet. Dust from the stars.

By now, Ken and his companions had learned the use of the electron microscope and how to prepare specimens for it. When their samples of dust had become sufficient they prepared a dozen slides for photographing with the instrument.

As these were at last developed in the darkroom, Ken scanned them eagerly. Actually, he did not know what he was looking for. None of them did. The prints seemed to show little more than shapeless patches. In the light of the laboratory he called Joe Walton's attention to one picture. "Look," he said. "Ever see anything like that before?"

Joe started to shake his head. Then he gave an exclamation. "Hey, they look like the same particles found in the metals, which nobody has been able to identify yet!"

Ken nodded. "It could be. Maybe this will get us only a horselaugh for our trouble, but let's see what they think."

They went into the next laboratory and laid the prints before Ken's father and his associates. Ken knew at once, from the expressions on the men's faces, that they were not going to be laughed at.

"I think there may be something here," said Professor Maddox, trying to suppress his excitement. "It is very difficult to tell in a picture like this whether one particle is similar to any other, but their size and configuration are very much alike."

Professor Douglas grunted disdainfully. "Impossible!" With that dismissal, he moved away.

Professor Larsen looked more carefully. "You could scrape dust from a thousand different sources and get pictures like this from half of them perhaps. Only the chemical tests will show us the nature of this material. I am certain it is very worthwhile following up."

"I feel certain that whatever contaminating agent we are dealing with is airborne," said Professor Maddox. "If this is the same substance it will not tell us its origin, of course, nor will it even prove it is responsible for these effects. However it is a step in the right direction. We can certainly stand that!"

"Couldn't we tell by spectroscopic analysis?" said Ken.

"That would be difficult to say. The commonness of the elements involved might mask what you are looking for. Get John Vickers to help you set up equipment for making some comparisons."

Vickers was the teaching fellow in the chemistry department whom Professor Maddox had planned to assign to help the boys when they first suggested atmospheric analysis. He had become indispensable in the research since then. But he liked helping the boys; it was not too long since he had been at the same stage in his own career. He understood their longing to do something worthwhile, and their embarrassment at their ineptness.

"Sure, Guys," he said, when Professor Maddox called him in. "Let's see if we can find out what this stuff is. Who knows? Maybe we've got a bear by the tail."

It was delicate precision work, preparing specimens and obtaining spectrographs of the lines that represented the elements contained in them. Time after time, their efforts failed. Something went wrong either with their sample preparation, or with their manipulation of the instruments. Ken began to feel as if their hands possessed nothing but thumbs.

"That's the way it goes," John Vickers consoled them. "Half of this business of being a scientist is knowing how to screw a nut on a left-handed bolt in the dark. Unless you're one of these guys who do it all in their heads, like Einstein."

"We're wasting our samples," Ken said. "It's taken two weeks to collect this much."

"Then this is the one that does it," said Vickers. "Try it now."

Ken turned the switch that illuminated the spectrum and exposed the photographic plate. After a moment, he cut it off. "That had better do it!" he said.

After the plates were developed, they had two successful spectrographs for comparison. One was taken from the metal of a failed-engine part. The other was from the atmospheric dust. In the comparator Vickers brought the corresponding standard comparison lines together. For a long time he peered through the eyepiece.

"A lot of lines match up," he said. "I can throw out most of them, though—carbon, oxygen, a faint sodium."

"The stuff that's giving us trouble might be a compound of one of these," said Ken.

"That's right. If so, we ought to find matching lines of other possible elements in the compounds concerned. I don't see any reasonable combination at all." He paused. "Hey, here's something I hadn't noticed."

He shifted the picture to the heavy end of the spectrum. There, a very sharp line matched on both pictures. The boys took a look at it through the viewer. "What is that one?" Ken asked.

"I don't know. I used a carbon standard. I should have used one farther toward the heavy end. This one looks like it would have to be a transuranic element, something entirely new, like plutonium."

"Then it could be from the hydrogen bomb tests," said Joe.

"It could be," said Vickers, "but somehow I've got a feeling it isn't."

"Isn't there a quick way to find out?" said Ken.

"How?"

"If we took a spectrograph of the comet and found this same line strongly present, we would have a good case for proving the comet was the source of this substance."

"Let's have a try," said Vickers. "I don't know how successfully we can get a spectrograph of the comet, but it's worth an attempt."

Their time was short, before the comet vanished below the horizon for the night. They called for help from the other boys and moved the equipment to the roof, using the small, portable 6-inch telescope belonging to the physics department.

There was time for only one exposure. After the sun had set, and the comet had dropped below the horizon, they came out of the darkroom and placed the prints in the viewing instrument.

Vickers moved the adjustments gently. After a time he looked up at the circle of boys. "You were right, Ken," he said. "Your hunch was right. The comet is responsible. Our engines have been stopped by dust from the stars."

8
ATTACK

There are people who feed upon disaster and grow in their own particular direction as they would never have grown without it, as does the queen bee who becomes queen only because of the special food prepared by the workers for her private use.

Such a man was Henry Maddox. He would not have admitted it, nor was he ever able to realize it, for it violated the very principles he had laid down for Ken. But for him, the comet was like a sudden burst of purpose in his life. He had taught well in his career as professor of chemistry at the State Agricultural College at Mayfield, but it had become fairly mechanical. He was vaguely aware of straining at the chains of routine from time to time, but he had always forced himself through sheer exercise of will to attend to his duties. There was never time, however, for any of the research he used to tell himself, in his younger days, he was going to do.

With the sudden thrusting aside of all customary duties, and with the impact of catastrophe demanding a solution to a research problem, he came alive without knowing what was happening. Yet without the imminence of disaster he would not have found the strength to drive himself so. This was what he could not admit to himself.

Another who was nourished was Granny Wicks. She should have been dead years ago. She had admitted this to herself and to anyone else who would listen, but now she knew why she had been kept alive so long past her time. She had been waiting for the comet.

Its energy seemed to flow from the sky into her withered, bony frame, and she drank of its substance until time seemed to reverse itself in her obsolete body. All her life she had been waiting for this time. She knew it now. She was spared to tell the people why the comet had come. Although her purpose was diametrically opposed to that of Henry Maddox, she also fed and grew to her full stature after almost a century of existence.

Frank Meggs was surely another. He was born in Mayfield and had lived there all his life and he hated every minute of time and every person and every event that told of his wasted life here. He hated College Hill, for he had never been able to go there. His family had been too poor, and he had been forced to take over his father's store when his father died.

He had once dreamed of becoming a great businessman and owning a chain of stores that would stretch from coast to coast, but circumstances, for which he blamed the whole of Mayfield, had never permitted him to leave the town. His panic sale had been his final, explosive hope that he might be able to make it. Now, he, too, found himself growing in his own special direction as he fed upon the disaster. He did not know just what that direction was or to where it led, but he felt the growth. He felt the secret pleasure of contemplating the discomfort and the privation that lay ahead for his fellow citizens in the coming months.

While personal fear forced him to the conclusion that the disaster would be of short duration, the pleasure was nevertheless real. It was especially intense when he thought of College Hill and its inhabitants in scenes of dark dismay as they wrestled in vain to understand what had happened to the world.

There were others who fed upon the disaster. For the most part they found it an interruption to be met with courage, with faith, with whatever strength was inherent in them.

It was not a time of growth, however, for Reverend Aylesworth. It was the kind of thing for which he had been preparing all his life. Now he would test and verify the stature he had already gained.

* * * * *

On the night they verified the presence of the comet dust in the disabled engines, Ken was the last to leave the laboratory. It was near midnight when he got away.

His father had left much earlier, urging him to come along, but Ken had been unable to pull himself away from the examination and measurement of the spectrum of lines that bared the comet's secret. He had begun to understand the pleasure his father had spoken of, the pleasure of being consumed utterly by a problem important in its own right.

As he left the campus there was no moon in the sky. The comet was gone, and the stars seemed new in a glory he had not seen for many nights. He felt that he wouldn't be able to sleep even when he got home, and he continued walking for several blocks, in the direction of town.

He came abreast, finally, of the former Rainbow Skating Rink, which had been converted into a food warehouse. In the darkness, he saw a sudden, swift movement against the wall of the building. His night vision was sharp after the long walk; he saw what was going on.

The broad doors of the rink had been broken open. There were three or four men lifting sacks and boxes and barrels stealthily into a wagon.

Even as he started toward them he realized his own foolishness and pulled back. A horse whinnied softly. He turned to run in the direction of Sheriff Johnson's house, and behind him came a sudden, hoarse cry of alarm.

Horses' hoofs rattled frighteningly loud on the cement. Ken realized he stood no chance of escaping if he were seen. He dodged for an instant into a narrow space between two buildings with the thought of reaching an alley at the back. However, it was boarded at the end and he saw that he would have to scale the fence. A desperate horseman would ride him down in the narrow space.

He fled on and reached the shadows in front of the drugstore. He pressed himself as flat as possible in the recess of the doorway, hoping his pursuer would race by. But his fleeing shadow had been seen.

The rider whirled and reined the horse to a furious stop. The animal's front legs pawed the air in front of Ken's face. Then Ken saw there was something familiar about the figure. He peered closer as the horseman whirled again.

"Jed," he called softly. "Jed Tucker—"

The figure answered harshly, "Yeah. Yeah, that's me, and you're—you're Ken. I'm sorry it had to be you. Why did you have to come by here at this time of night?"

Ken heard the sound of running feet in the distance as others came to join Jed Tucker. Jed had not dismounted, but held Ken prisoner in the recess with the rearing, impatient horse.

Ken wondered how Jed Tucker could be mixed up in a thing like this. His father was president of the bank and owned one of the best homes in Mayfield. Jed and Ken had played football on the first team together last year.

"Jed," Ken said quickly, "give it up! Don't go through with this!"

"Shut up!" Jed snarled. He reined the horse nearer, threatening Ken with the thrashing front legs.

When Jed's companions arrived, Jed dismounted from the horse.

"Who is it?" a panting voice asked.

A cold panic shot through Ken. He recognized the voice. It was that of Mr. Tucker himself. The bank official was taking part in the looting of the warehouse.

The third man, Ken recognized in rising horror, was Mr. Allen, a next-door neighbor of the Tuckers. He was the town's foremost attorney, and one of its most prominent citizens.

"We can't let him go," Allen was saying. "Whoever he is, we've got to get him out of the way."

Mr. Tucker came closer. He gasped in dismay. "It's young Maddox," he said. "You! What are you doing out this time of night?"

Under any other conditions, the question would have seemed humorous, coming from whom it did now. But Ken felt no humor; he sensed the desperate fury in these men.

"Give it up," he repeated quietly. "The lives of fifteen thousand people depend on this food supply. You have no right to steal an ounce that doesn't belong to you. I'll never tell what I've seen."

Tucker shook his head in a dazed, uncomprehending manner, as if the proposition were too fantastic to be considered. "We can't do that," he said.

"We can't let him go!" Allen repeated.

"You can't expect us to risk murder!"

"There'll be plenty of that before this winter's over!"

"Our lives depend on this food, you know that," Tucker said desperately to Ken. "You take your share, and we'll all be in this together. Then we know we'll be safe."

Ken considered, his panic increasing. To refuse might mean his life. If he could pretend to fall in with them....

"You can't trust him!" Allen raged. "No one is going to be in on this except us."

Suddenly the lawyer stepped near, his hand raised high in the air. Before Ken sensed his intention, a heavy club smashed against his head. His body fell in a crumpled heap on the sidewalk.

*   *   *   *   *

It was after 2 a.m. when Professor Maddox awoke with the sensation that something was vaguely wrong. He sat up in bed and looked out the window at the starlit sky. He remembered he had left Ken at the university and had not yet heard him come in.

Quietly he arose from the bed and tiptoed along the hallway to Ken's room. He used the beam of a precious flashlight for a moment to scan the undisturbed bed. Panic started inside him and was fought down.

Probably Ken had found something interesting to keep him from noticing the alarm clock on a shelf in the laboratory. Perhaps someone had even forgotten to wind the clock and it had run down.

Perhaps, even, the bearings of its balance wheel had finally become frozen and had brought it to a stop!

Mrs. Maddox was behind him as he turned from the door. "What's wrong?" she asked.

He flashed the light on the bed again. "I'd better go up to the laboratory and have a look," he said.

Ken's mother nodded. She sensed her husband's worry, and wanted not to add to it. "Take Ken's bicycle," she said. "It will be quicker, even if you have to walk it uphill. I'll have some hot chocolate for you when you come back."

Professor Maddox dressed hurriedly and took the bicycle from the garage. He did have to wheel it most of the way up the hill, but it would be easier coming down anyway, he thought. He wondered how much longer the bearings in it would hold up without freezing.

As he came within view of the laboratory building he saw that the windows were utterly dark. He knew that even with the shades down he would have been able to see some glow of the oil lamps which they used, provided Ken were still there.

He waited a full 10 minutes against the chance that Ken had put out the lamps and was on his way out. Then he knew Ken had gone long ago. He ought to call the

Sheriff and have the police cars search for him, but there were no phones and no cars.

He mounted the bicycle in fresh panic and rode recklessly down the hill to town. At Sheriff Johnson's house he pounded frantically on the door until the Sheriff shouted angrily through an open window, "Who is it?"

"It's Dr. Maddox. You've got to help me, Johnson. Ken's disappeared." He went into details, and the Sheriff grunted, holding back his irritation at being disturbed, because of his long friendship with Henry Maddox.

"I guess I should have gone down to the station," said Professor Maddox, realizing what he had done. "I had forgotten there would be men on duty."

"It's all right. I'll come with you."

The Sheriff's car had broken down days before. He kept a horse for his own official use. "You can ride behind me," he said. "Sally's a pretty decent gal. You get up there on the porch railing and climb on right behind me."

Professor Maddox maneuvered himself behind the Sheriff on the horse, balancing unsteadily as Sally shied away. "Where do you think Ken could have gone?" asked Johnson. "Don't you suppose he's over at one of his friend's?"

"He wouldn't do a thing like that without letting us know."

"He went up the canyon with the wood detail 2 or 3 weeks ago."

"I know—but that was different. Aren't there any policemen on the streets now? What happened to the ones who used to patrol in the radio cars?"

"They're walking their beats, most of them. Two are mounted in each district. We'll stop by the station, and then try to find the mounted officers. It's the only thing we can do."

They moved down the dark, empty streets. It seemed as if there never had been any life flowing along them, and never would be again. They passed the station, lit by a smoking oil lamp, and left word of Ken's disappearance, and moved on. They came to the edge of the business section, where street lamps used to shine. This area was even more ghostly than the rest, but policemen patrolled it, perhaps out of habit and a conviction that failure to do so would admit the end of all that was familiar and right.

As they rode on, the clatter of other hoofbeats on the cement sounded behind them. Johnson turned and halted. A flashlight shone in their faces. It was Officer Dan Morris, who identified himself by turning the light on his own face.

"The warehouse has been broken into," he said. "Over at the skating rink. Somebody has busted in and made off with a lot of food."

The Sheriff seemed stunned by the news. "What idiots!" he muttered self-accusingly. "What complete, pinheaded idiots we turned out to be. We didn't even think to put a special guard around the warehouse! Do any of the other patrolmen know?"

"Yes. Clark and Dudly are over there now. I was trying to round up someone else while they look for clues."

"I'll have to get over there," said Johnson.

"But Ken ..." Professor Maddox said. "I've got to keep looking."

"You come with us. I've got to look into the robbery. Ken can't have come to any harm. I'll pass the word along and we'll all keep watch for him. I promise you we will."

"I'll keep on," said Professor Maddox. He slid from the horse. "I'll keep moving along the street here. If you find anything, I'll be somewhere between here and home."

Unwillingly, Sheriff Johnson turned and left him. The sounds of the two horses echoed loudly in the deserted street. Professor Maddox felt a burst of anger at their abandonment of him, but he supposed the Sheriff was doing what he had to do.

He recognized that it was foolhardy to be afoot in the deserted town this time of night. Without a single clue to

Ken's whereabouts, what could he hope to accomplish? He strode on along the sidewalk in the direction the policeman had disappeared. It was as good a direction as any.

After he had gone a block he stumbled in the darkness. Some soft, resilient object lay across the sidewalk before Billings Drugstore. In anger at the obstacle, Professor Maddox caught himself and moved on. A sound stopped him. A groan of agony came from the object upon which he had stumbled. He turned and bent down and knew it was a human being. Faintly, under the starlight, he glimpsed the dark pool of blood on the sidewalk. He turned the body gently until he could see the face. It was Ken.

He didn't know how long he knelt there inspecting the motionless features of his son. He was aware only of running frantically in the direction of the warehouse. He found Johnson. He clutched the Sheriff's arm. "They've killed him!" he cried. "I found Ken and they've killed him!"

Johnson turned to the nearest officer. "Ride for Dr. Adams. Dudly, get that horse and wagon that's at Whitaker's place. Where did you say you found Ken, Professor?"

"At Billings. Lying on the sidewalk with his head smashed in."

"You others meet us there," he called.

Clumsily, they mounted the Sheriff's horse together again. It seemed to take hours to ride the short distance.

They dismounted and Johnson knelt and touched the boy tenderly.

Then Professor Maddox heard, barely audible, the sound he would remember all his life as the most wonderful sound in the world.

"Dad...." Ken's lips moved with the word. "Dad...." His voice was a plea for help.

9
JUDGMENT

There was snow. It covered the whole world beyond the hospital window. Its depth was frightening, and the walls seemed no barrier. It was as much inside as out, filling the room to the ceiling with a fluffy white that swirled and pulsed in waves before his eyes.

Much later, when the pain softened and his vision cleared, he saw the only real snow was that piled outside almost to the level of the first-story windows. Within the room, the outline of familiar objects showed clearly.

In half-recovered consciousness he wondered impersonally about the dying pain in his head and how he came to be where he was. He could remember only about a strange thing in the sky, and a great fear.

Then it burst upon him in full recollection—the comet, the dust, the laboratory. They had proved the dust that was in the comet's tail had accumulated in the metal surfaces of the failed engines. What more did they need to prove the comet's responsibility?

He slept, and when he awoke his father was there. "Hi, Son," Professor Maddox said.

Ken smiled weakly. "Hi, Dad."

Dr. Adams wouldn't let them talk much, and he didn't want Ken's father to tell him why he was there. He wanted Ken to dredge out of his own memories the circumstances of the attack.

Ken said, "I've got to get out of here. Things must be getting behind at the lab. Have you found anything new?"

"Take it easy," his father said. "We've got a little better picture of what we're up against. The dust is quite

definitely from the comet's tail. It has a very large
molecule, and is suspended in our atmosphere in colloidal
form. Its basis is a transuranic element, which is,
however, only slightly radioactive. By volume, it is
present in the amount of about one part in ten million,
which is fairly heavy concentration for an alien substance
of that kind.

"Perhaps the most important thing we've found is that
it has a strong affinity for metals, so that its
accumulation on metallic surfaces is much higher than in
the general atmosphere."

"It would!" Ken said, with a vague attempt at humor.
"Why couldn't it have had an affinity for old rubber tires,
or secondhand galoshes?

"How late is it? Can I get up to the lab this
afternoon?" Ken struggled to a sitting position. A gigantic
pain shot through his head and down his spinal column.
He felt as if his head were encased in a cement block. He
fell back with a groan.

"Don't try that again for a few days!" his father said
severely. "You're not going anywhere for quite a while. I
have to go now, but your mother will be in tonight. Maria
will come, too. You do what the doctors and nurses tell
you to!"

"Dad—why am I here?" He moaned in agony of both
spirit and body.

"You had an accident," said Dr. Adams smoothly. "It
will all come back to you and you'll soon be fine."

Ken watched his father disappear through the
doorway. He felt the sting of a needle in his arm and was
aware the nurse was standing near. He wanted to talk
some more, but suddenly he was too tired to do anything.

*   *   *   *   *

It came to him in the middle of the night, like a dark,
wild dream that could be only the utmost fantasy. He
remembered the silent, shapeless figures against the

black wall of the old skating rink, and then he knew it wasn't a dream because he could remember clearly the words of Jed Tucker and his father. He could also remember Mr. Allen saying, "We can't let him go. Whoever he is, we've got to get him out of the way."

He remembered the instant of crashing pain. Mr. Allen had struck with the intent to kill him. Again, he wondered for a moment if it were not just a nightmare. Mr. Allen, the town's leading attorney, and Mr. Tucker, the banker–what would they be doing, plotting robbery and killing?

In the morning he told his father about it. Professor Maddox could not believe it, either. "You must be mistaken, Ken," he protested. "These men are two of our leading citizens. They're both on the Mayor's food committee. You suffered a pretty terrible shock, and you'll have to realize the effects of it may be with you, and may upset your thinking, for quite a while."

"Not about this! I know who it was. I recognized their voices in the dark. Jed Tucker admitted his identity when I called his name. If there's anything gone from the warehouse, Sheriff Johnson will find it in their possession."

The Sheriff had to wait for permission from Dr. Adams, but he came around that afternoon, and was equally unbelieving. He advanced the same arguments Professor Maddox had used about the character of those Ken accused.

"These men will do something far worse, if you don't stop them," said Ken.

"He's right, there," said Professor Maddox. "Those who did this, menace the whole community. They've got to be found."

"We'll make fools of ourselves," said the Sheriff, "if we go to Tucker's and Allen's, and demand to search the premises. We've got to have more than your word, Ken;

some evidence of their positive connection with the crime."

"I just know I saw and heard them. That's all."

"Listen," the Sheriff said suddenly, "there's one man in this town that's really out to get you: Frank Meggs. Don't you think it could be Meggs and some of his friends?"

"No. It wasn't Frank Meggs."

*   *   *   *   *

Art Matthews came around later that same day. "You look worse than one of these engines that's got itself full of stardust," he said. "You must have been off your rocker, prowling around back alleys in the middle of the night!"

Ken grinned. "Hi, Art. I knew you'd be full of sympathy. What's going on outside while I've been laid up? Say–I don't even know how long I've been here! What day is it?"

"Tuesday. Not that it makes any difference any more."

"Tuesday–and it was Saturday when I was working with the spectroscope. I've been here three days!"

"A week and three days," said Art Matthews. "You were out cold for three days straight, and they wondered if your bearings were ever going to turn again."

Ken lay back in astonishment. "Nobody's told me anything. What's happening outside?"

"It's going to be a rough winter," Art Matthews said, grimly. "Snow's started heavy, two weeks earlier than usual. I understand Professor Douglas thinks it's got something to do with the comet dust in the air."

"That figures. What about the fuel supply?"

"In pretty sad shape, too. So far, the stockpile is big enough for about a week and a half of real cold. They laid off woodcutting for three days to spend all the time converting oil burners, and making new heaters out of 50-

gallon barrels and anything else they could find. It's going to be a mighty cold winter–and a hungry one."

Ken nodded, but he seemed to be thinking of something else.

"I've had an idea," he said. "How's your stock of spare parts in the garage?"

"Good. I always was a fool about stocking up on things I could never sell."

"Any blocks?"

"About a dozen, why?"

"Could you make a brand-new engine out of spare parts?"

The mechanic considered, then nodded. "I think I could put together a Ford or Chevy engine. What good would that do? It would run down in a few days, just like all the rest."

"Do you think it would, if you put it in a sealed room, and supplied only filtered air to it?"

Art's eyes lighted. "Why the dickens didn't we think of that before? If we could keep the stardust from getting to the engine, there's no reason at all why it shouldn't run as long as we wanted it to, is there?"

"If a generator could be assembled in the same way, we could stir up a little power on an experimental basis, enough to charge our radio batteries. I wonder how much power could be generated in the whole country by such means?"

"I know we could get a couple of dozen engines going here in Mayfield, at least!" said Art.

"Why don't you get started right away? Get some of the club guys to help. If that filter idea works there may be a lot of things we can do."

Art started for the door. "Sheer genius," he said admiringly. "That's sheer genius, Boy!"

Ken smiled to himself. He wondered why they hadn't tried that when they first had the hunch that comet dust could be responsible. Maybe they could have saved some of the cars if they had rigged more efficient filters on the air intakes.

His thoughts went back to the attack. He was still thinking about it when his father and Sheriff Johnson returned.

"We took your word, Son," the Sheriff said, chagrined. "We got a warrant and searched the Tucker and Allen premises from top to bottom. We went out to Tucker's farm and went through the barns and the house. They've got a 2-day supply of rations just like everybody else.

"They screamed their heads off and threatened suit for slander and false arrest and everything else in the books."

"I'll get hold of Jed Tucker when I get out of here," said Ken. "He'll talk when I get through with him!"

"Don't get yourself in a worse jam than you've stirred up already. Unless you can prove what you say, you'll just have to forget it and keep quiet."

Ken smiled suddenly. "It just occurred to me—when a banker wants to keep something safe, where does he put it?"

"In the bank, of course," said the Sheriff. "Wait a minute, you don't think...."

"Why not? The bank isn't doing business any more. Tucker is the only one, probably, who has any excuse to go down there. As long as things are the way they are, nobody else is going to get inside the vault—or even inside the building."

Professor Maddox and the Sheriff looked at each other. "It's a logical idea," said Ken's father.

"It's as crazy as the rest of it! We've made fools of ourselves already so we might as well finish the job!"

*   *   *   *   *

When breakfast was served the next morning, Ken found out his hunch had been right. He heard it from

Miss Haskins the nurse and knew, therefore, that it must be all over town.

The nurse was wide-eyed. "What do you think?" she said, as she set out the bowl of oatmeal. "The Sheriff found that Mr. Tucker had filled his bank vault with food. He'd stolen it from the warehouse. The Sheriff's men obtained a warrant and forced Tucker to open the vault, and there were cases of canned goods stacked clear to the ceiling!"

"He must have been afraid of getting hungry," said Ken.

"To think a man like Mr. Tucker would do something like that!" She went out, clucking her tongue in exaggerated dismay.

Ken leaned back with satisfaction. He quite agreed with Miss Haskins. It was a pretty awful thing for a man like Mr. Tucker to have done.

How many others would do far worse before the winter was over?

* * * * *

The sun came out bright and clear after the series of heavy snowstorms. The comet added its overwhelming, golden light and tinted the world of snow. Some of the snow was melted by the tantalizing warmth, but water that had melted in the daytime froze immediately at night, and the unequal contest between the elements could have only one outcome in a prematurely cold and miserable winter.

As the pain in his head dwindled, and he was able to get about in the hospital, Ken grew more and more impatient to be released. He wondered about the heating and other facilities in the hospital and learned the Mayor's committee had ordered one wing kept open at all times, with heat and food available to care for any emergency cases.

Three days after he was allowed on his feet, Ken was told by Dr. Adams that he could be released for the hearing of the Tuckers and Mr. Allen.

Ken stared at him. "I don't want to go to any hearing! I'm going back to the laboratory!"

"You can go home," said Dr. Adams. "I want you to rest a few more days, and then I would prefer seeing you get out in the open, working with the wood crew, instead of going right back to the lab.

"As for the trial and hearing, I'm afraid you have no choice. Judge Rankin has postponed the hearing so that you could appear, and he'll issue a subpoena if necessary to insure your presence."

"They caught Tucker redhanded with his bank vault stuffed to the ceiling with stolen goods. They don't need me!"

"They tried to kill you," Dr. Adams reminded him. "That's quite different from robbing a warehouse."

"I'm not interested in their punishment. It's more important to work on the analysis of the comet dust."

But there was no way out of it. Judge Rankin ordered Ken to appear. In spite of the fact that the building was unheated, and mushy snow was falling from a heavy sky once more, the courtroom was jammed on the day of the hearing.

Ken raged inwardly at the enormous waste of human resources. Men who should have been in the hills gathering wood, women who should have been at work on clothing and food projects were there to feed on the carcasses of the reputations presently to be destroyed.

Ken had little difficulty feeling sorry for Jed. His former teammate had been a good sport in all Ken's experience of playing with him. He could almost feel pity for Jed's father, too. On the stand, the banker looked steadfastly at the floor as he answered questions in a dull, monotone voice. He admitted the theft of the warehouse goods.

Judge Rankin asked severely, "Why, Mr. Tucker? Why did you think you had any more right to hoard supplies than the rest of us?"

For the first time the banker looked up, and he met the judge's eyes. "We were scared," he said simply. "We were scared of what is going to happen this winter."

The judge's eyes flashed. "So you were scared?" he cried. "Don't you think we're all scared?"

The banker shook his head and looked at the floor. "I don't know," he said, as if in a daze. "We were just scared."

The lawyer, Allen, was more belligerent when he took the stand. "We merely did what anyone else in this courtroom would do if he had the chance, and thought of it first," he said. "Do with me what you like, but before this winter is over, I'll see you self-righteous citizens of Mayfield at each other's throats for a scrap of food."

He admitted the attack on Ken, but denied the intent to kill.

When Ken's turn came, he told his story as simply and as quickly as possible, and when he had finished he said, "I'd like to add one more word, if I may."

The judge nodded. "Go ahead, Ken."

He looked over the faces of the audience. "We've got troubles enough," he said slowly. "As much as we hate to admit it, the picture Mr. Allen gives us may be right— unless we do what we can to stop it.

"We're wasting time and resources today. My father and I should be at the laboratory. Every man and woman here is neglecting a job. We waste time, deliberating about punishment for some of our neighbors who are perhaps weaker, but certainly no more frightened than the rest of us. If we lock them up in prison somebody has to watch out for them, and the whole community is deprived of their useful labor.

"Why don't we just let them go?"

A gasp of surprise came from the spectators, but a slow illumination seemed to light the face of Judge Rankin. His eyes moved from Ken to the accused men and then to the audience.

"This court has just heard what it considers some very sound advice," he said. "Jed, Mr. Tucker, Mr. Allen...."

The three stood before him.

"I am taking it upon myself, because of the emergency conditions that confront us, to declare that the penalty for your crime is continued and incessant labor at any task the community may see fit to assign you. You are marked men. Your crime is known to every member of this community. There will be no escape from the surveillance of your neighbors and friends. I sentence you to so conduct yourselves in the eyes of these people that, if we do come through this time of crisis, you may stand redeemed for all time of the crime which you have committed.

"If you fail to do this, the punishment which will be automatically imposed is banishment from this community for the duration of the emergency.

"Court stands adjourned!"

A burst of cheers broke out in the room. The Tuckers and Mr. Allen looked as if they could not believe what they had heard. Then Jed turned suddenly and rushed toward Ken.

"It's no good saying I've been a fool, but let me say thanks for your help."

Mr. Tucker took Ken's other hand. "You'll never regret it, young man. I'll see to it that you never regret it."

"It's okay," said Ken, almost gruffly. "We've all got a lot of work to do."

He turned as a figure brushed by them. Mr. Allen pushed through the crowd to the doorway. He looked at no one.

"We were fools," said Mr. Tucker bitterly. "Brainless, scared fools."

When they were gone, Dr. Aylesworth put his hand on Ken's shoulder. "That was a mighty fine thing you did. I hope it sets a pattern for all of us in times to come."

"I didn't do it for them," said Ken. "I did it for myself."

The minister smiled and clapped the boy's shoulder again. "Nevertheless, you did it. That's what counts."

10
VICTORY OF THE DUST

By the time Ken was through with the ordeal in court, Art Matthews had succeeded in building an engine from entirely new parts. He had it installed in an airtight room into which only filtered air could pass.

This room, and another air filter, had been major projects in themselves. The science club members had done most of the work after their daily stint at the laboratory, while Art had scoured the town for parts that would fit together.

At the end of the hearing Ken went to the garage. The engine had been running for 5 hours then. Art was grinning like a schoolboy who had just won a spelling bee. "She sure sounds sweet," he said. "I'll bet we can keep her going as long as we have gasoline."

"I hope so," Ken said. "It's just a waste of power to let it run that way, though."

Art scratched his head. "Yeah. It's funny, power is what we've been wanting, and now we've got a little we don't know what to do with it."

"Let's see if we can find a generator," said Ken. "Charge some batteries with it. Do you think there's one in town?"

"The best deal I can think of would be to scrounge a big motor, say an elevator motor, and convert it. The one belonging to the 5-story elevator in the Norton Building is our best bet. I don't imagine it froze up before the power went out."

"Let's get it then," said Ken. "Shut this off until we're ready to use it. To be on the safe side, could you cast some new bearings for the generator?"

"I don't see why not."

When he returned home Ken told his father for the first time about the project Art was working on.

"It sounds interesting," Professor Maddox said. "I'm not sure exactly what it will prove."

Ken slumped in the large chair in the living room, weak after his exertions of the day. "It would mean that if we could find enough unfrozen engines, or could assemble them from spare parts, we could get some power equipment in operation again.

"However, as Art said about this one engine, what good is it? Dad—even if we lick this problem, how are things ever going to get started up again?"

"What do you mean?"

"We've got one automobile engine going. Pretty soon we'll run out of gas here in Mayfield. Where do we get more? We can't until the railroad can haul it, or the pipelines can pump it. What happens when the stock at the refineries is all used up? How can they get into operation again? They need power for their own plant, electricity for their pumps and engines. All of their frozen equipment has to be replaced. Maybe some of it will have to be manufactured. How do the factories and plants get started again?"

"I don't know the answers to all that," Ken's father said. "Licking the comet dust *is* only half the problem— and perhaps the smallest half, at that. Our economy and industry will have to start almost from scratch in getting underway. How that will come about, if it ever does, I do not know."

To conserve their ration of firewood, only a small blaze burned in the fireplace. The kitchen and living room were being heated by it alone. The rest of the house was closed off.

"We ought to rig up something else," Ken said tiredly. "That wastes too much heat. What's Mom cooking on?"

"Mayor Hilliard found a little wood burner and gave it to me. I haven't had time to try converting our oil furnace."

Ken felt unable to stay awake longer. He went upstairs to bed for a few hours. Later, his mother brought a dinner tray. "Do you want it here, or would you rather come down where it's warm?" she asked.

"I'll come down. I want to get up for a while."

"Maria is out in the shack. She has a scheduled contact with Berkeley, but she says the transmitter won't function. It looks like a burned-out tube to her. She wanted to call Joe."

Ken scrambled out of bed and grabbed for his clothes. "I'll take care of it. Save dinner for me. We've got to keep the station on the air, no matter what happens!"

He found Maria seated by the desk, listening to the Berkeley operator's repeated call, to which she could not reply. The girl wore a heavy cardigan sweater, which was scarcely sufficient for the cold in the room. The small, tin-can heater was hardly noticeable.

Maria looked up as Ken burst through the doorway. "I didn't want you to come," she said. "They could have called Joe."

"We can't risk disturbing our schedule. They might think we've gone under and we'd lose our contact completely."

Hastily he examined the tube layout and breathed a sigh of relief when he saw it was merely one of the 801's that had burned a filament. They had a good stock of spares. He replaced the tube and closed the transmitter cage. After the tubes had warmed up, and the Berkeley operator paused to listen for their call, Ken picked up the microphone and threw in the antenna switch.

"Mayfield calling Berkeley." He repeated this several times. "Our transmitter's been out with a bum bottle. Let

us know if you read us now." He repeated again and
switched back to the receiver.

The Berkeley operator's voice indicated his relief. "I
read you, Mayfield. I hoped you hadn't gone out of
commission. The eggheads here seem to think your
Maddox-Larsen combination is coming up with more dope
on comet dust than anybody else in the country."

Ken grinned and patted himself and Maria on the
back. "That's us," he said. She grimaced at him.

"Hush!" she said.

"I've got a big report here from Dr. French. Confirm if
you're ready to tape it, and I'll let it roll."

Maria cut in to confirm that they were receiving and
ready to record. The Berkeley operator chuckled as he
came back. "That's the one I like to hear," he said. "That
'Scandahoovian' accent is real cute. Just as soon as things
get rolling again I'm coming out there to see what else
goes with it."

"He's an idiot," Maria said.

"But probably a pretty nice guy," Ken said.

They listened carefully as the Berkeley operator read
a number of pages of reports by Dr. French and his
associates, concerning experiments run in the university
laboratories. These gave Ken a picture of the present
stage of the work on the comet dust. He felt disheartened.
Although the material had been identified as a colloidal
compound of a new, transuranic metal, no one had yet
been able to determine its exact chemical structure nor
involve it in any reaction that would break it down.

It seemed to Ken that one of the biggest drawbacks
was lack of sufficient sample material to work with.
Everything they were doing was by micromethods. He
supposed it was his own lack of experience and his
clumsiness in the techniques that made him feel he was
always working in the dark when trying to analyze
chemical specimens that were barely visible.

When the contact was completed and the stations
signed off, Maria told Ken what she had heard over the

air during the time he was in the hospital. Several other amateur operators in various parts of the country had heard them with their own battery-powered sets. They had asked to join in an expanded news net.

Joe and Al had agreed to this, and Ken approved as he heard of it. "It's a good idea. I was hoping to reach some other areas. Maybe we can add some industrial laboratories to our net if any are still operating."

"We've got three," said Maria. "General Electric in Schenectady, General Motors in Detroit, and Hughes in California. Amateurs working for these companies called in. They're all working on the dust."

Through these new amateur contacts Maria had learned that Chicago had been completely leveled by fire. Thousands had died in the fire and in the rioting that preceded it.

New York City had suffered almost as much, although no general fire had broken out. Mob riots over the existing, scanty food supplies had taken thousands of lives. Other thousands had been lost in a panicky exodus from the city. The highways leading into the farming areas in upstate New York and New England areas were clogged with starving refugees. Thousands of huddled bodies lay under the snow.

Westward into Pennsylvania and south into Delaware it was the same. Here the refugees were met with other streams of desperate humanity moving out of the thickly populated cities. Epidemics of disease had broken out where the starving population was thickest and the sanitary facilities poorest.

On the west coast the situation was somewhat better. The population of the Bay Area was streaming north and south toward Red Bluff and Sacramento, and into the Salinas and San Joaquin valleys. From southern California they were moving east to the reclaimed desert farming areas. There were suffering and death among them, but the rioting and mob violence were less.

From all over the country there were increasing reports of groups of wanderers moving like nomadic tribesmen, looting, killing, and destroying. There was no longer any evidence of a central government capable of sufficient communication to control these elements of the population on even a local basis.

Maria played the tapes of these reports for Ken. She seemed stolid and beyond panic as she heard them again. To Ken, hearing them for the first time, it seemed utterly beyond belief. It was simply some science-fiction horror story played on the radio or television, and when it was over he would find the world was completely normal.

He looked up and saw Maria watching him. He saw the little tin-can stove with a few sticks of green wood burning ineffectively. He saw the large rack of batteries behind the transmitter. Unexpectedly, for the first time in many days, he thought of the Italian steamship alone in the middle of the Atlantic.

"The *White Bird*," he said to Maria. "Did you hear anything more of her?"

"One of the amateurs told me he'd picked up a report from the ship about a week ago. The radio operator said he was barricaded in the radio room. Rioting had broken out all over the ship. Dozens of passengers had been killed; the ones who were left were turning cannibalistic. That was the last report anyone has heard from the ship."

Ken shuddered. He glanced through the window and caught a vision of Science Hall on College Hill. A fortress, he thought. There were maybe a dozen other such fortresses scattered throughout the world; in them lay the only hope against the enemy that rampaged across the Earth.

In the sky, he could see the comet's light faintly, even through the lead-gray clouds from which snow was falling.

"You should get back to bed," said Maria. "You look as if you had been hit two hours ago instead of two weeks."

"Yeah, I guess I'd better." Ken arose, feeling weak and dizzy. "Can you get that report typed for Dad tonight? It would be good for him to be able to take it to the lab with him in the morning."

"I'll get it done," said Maria. "You get off to bed."

As much as he rebelled against it, Ken was forced to spend the next two days in bed. Dr. Adams allowed him to be up no more than a few hours on the third day. "I'm afraid you took a worse beating than any of us thought," the doctor said. "You'll just have to coast for a while."

It was as he was finally getting out of bed again that he heard Art Matthews, when the mechanic came to the door and spoke with Ken's mother.

"This is awfully important," Art said. "I wish you'd ask him if he doesn't feel like seeing me for just a minute."

"He's had a bad relapse, and the doctor says he has to be kept very quiet for a day or two longer."

Dressed, except for his shoes, Ken went to the hall and leaned over the stair railing. "I'll be down in just a minute, Art. It's okay, Mom. I'm feeling good today."

"Ken! You shouldn't!" his mother protested.

In a moment he had his shoes on and was racing down the stairs. "What's happened, Art? Anything gone wrong?"

The mechanic looked downcast. "Everything! We got the Norton elevator motor and hooked it up with the gas engine. It ran fine for a couple of days, and we got a lot of batteries charged up."

"Then it quit," said Ken.

"Yeah–how did you know?"

"I've been afraid we had missed one bet. It just isn't enough to supply filtered air to the engines built of new parts. The parts themselves are already contaminated with the dust. As soon as they go into operation, we have the same old business, all over again.

"Unless some means of decontamination can be found these new parts are no better than the old ones."

"Some of these parts were wrapped in tissue paper and sealed in cardboard boxes!" Art protested. "How could enough dust get to them to ruin them?"

"The dust has a way of getting into almost any corner it wants to," said Ken. "Dad and the others have found it has a tremendous affinity for metals, so it seeps through cracks and sticks. It never moves off once it hits a piece of metal. What parts of the engine froze?"

"Pistons, bearings—just like all the rest."

"The generator shaft, too?"

Art nodded. "It might have gone a few more revolutions. It seemed loose when we started work, but as soon as we broke the bearings apart they seemed to fasten onto the shaft like they were alive. How do you account for that? The bearings were new; I just cast them yesterday."

"They were contaminated by dust between casting and installation in the protected room. We've got to dig a lot deeper before we've got the right answer. It might be worthwhile setting up another rig just like the one we have in order to get some more juice in our batteries. Do you think you could do it again, or even several times? That engine lasted about 90 hours, didn't it?"

"Eighty-eight, altogether. I suppose I could do it again if you think it's worth it. The trouble is getting generators. Maybe we could machine the shaft of this one and cast a new set of bearings to fit. I'll try if you think it's worth it."

"Get it ready to run," said Ken. "The battery power for our radio isn't going to last forever. We'll be in a real jam if we lose touch with the outside."

11
THE ANIMALS ARE SICK

That night, Ken reported to his father the fate of the engine assembled by Art.

"It did seem too good to be true," said Professor Maddox. He stretched wearily in the large chair by the feeble heat of the fireplace. "It bears out our observation of the affinity of the dust for metals."

"How is that?"

"It attaches itself almost like a horde of microscopic magnets. It literally burrows into the surface of the metal."

"You don't mean that!"

"I do. Its presence breaks down the surface tension, as we had supposed. The substance actually then works its way into the interstices of the molecules. As the colloid increases in quantity, its molecules loosen the bond between the molecules of the metal, giving them increased freedom of motion.

"This can be aggravated by frictional contacts, and finally we have the molecular interchange that binds the two pieces into one."

"The only metal that would be clean would be that which had been hermetically sealed since before the appearance of the comet," said Ken. "Look—wouldn't this affinity of the dust for metal provide a means of purifying the atmosphere? If we could run the air through large filters of metal wool, the dust would be removed!"

"Yes, I'm very sure we could do it that way. It would merely require that we run the atmosphere of the whole Earth through such a filter. Do you have any idea how that could be done?"

"It would work in the laboratory, but would be wholly impractical on a worldwide scale," Ken admitted. "How will we ever rid the atmosphere of the dust! A colloid will float forever in the air, even after the comet is gone."

"Exactly," Professor Maddox said, "and, as far as we are concerned, the whole atmosphere of the Earth is permanently poisoned. Our problem is to process it in some manner to remove that poison.

"During the past few days we have come to the conclusion that there are only two alternatives: One is to process the whole atmosphere by passing it through some device, such as the filter you have suggested. The second is to put some substance into the air which will counteract and destroy the dust, precipitate it out of the atmosphere."

"Since the first method is impractical what can be used in carrying out the second?"

"We've set ourselves the goal of discovering that. We're hoping to synthesize the necessary chemical compound to accomplish it."

"It would have to be a colloid, too, capable of suspension in the atmosphere," said Ken.

"Correct."

"If we do find such a substance we still have the problem of decontaminating existing metals. We couldn't build a moving piece of machinery out of any metal now in existence without first cleaning the dust out of its surface."

"That's part of the problem, too," said his father.

*   *   *   *   *

Ken resumed his duties in the laboratory the following morning. Dr. Adams had warned him not to walk up College Hill, so he had borrowed the horse Dave Whitaker still had on loan from his uncle. He felt self-conscious about being the only one enjoying such luxury, but he promised himself he would go back to walking as soon as Dr. Adams gave permission.

On the third day, the horse slipped and fell as it picked its way carefully down the hill. Ken was thrown clear, into the deep snow, but the horse lay where it had fallen, as if unable to move. Ken feared the animal had broken a leg. He felt cautiously but could find no evidence of injury.

Gently, he tugged at the reins and urged the horse to its feet. The animal finally rose, but it stood uncertainly and trembled when it tried to walk again.

Ken walked rather than rode the rest of the way home. He took the horse to the improvised stable beside the science shack. There he got out the ration of hay and water, and put a small amount of oats in the trough. The animal ignored the food and drink.

After dinner, Ken went out again to check. The horse was lying down in the stall and the food remained untouched.

Ken returned to the house and said to his father, "Dave's horse slipped today, and I'm afraid something serious is wrong with him. He doesn't seem to have any broken bones, but he won't eat or get up. I think I should go for the vet."

His father agreed. "We can't afford to risk a single horse, considering how precious they are now. You stay in the house and I'll go to Dr. Smithers' place myself."

Ken protested. He hated to see his father go out again on such a cold night.

Dr. Smithers grumbled when Professor Maddox reached his house and explained what he wanted. As one of the town's two veterinarians, he had been heavily overworked since the disaster struck. The slightest sign of injury or illness in an animal caused the Mayor's livestock committee to call for help.

"Probably nothing but a strained ligament," Smithers said. "You could have taken care of it by wrapping it yourself."

"We think you ought to come."

When the veterinarian finally reached the side of the animal, he inspected him carefully by the light of a gasoline lantern. The horse was lying on his side in a bed of hay; he was breathing heavily and his eyes were bright and glassy.

Dr. Smithers sucked his breath in sharply and bent closer. Finally, he got to his feet and stared out over the expanse of snow. "It couldn't be," he muttered. "We just don't deserve that. We don't deserve it at all."

"What is it?" Ken asked anxiously. "Is it something very serious?"

"I don't know for sure. It looks like–it could be anthrax. I'm just afraid that it is."

Dr. Smithers' eyes met and held Professor Maddox's. Ken did not understand. "I've heard that name, but I don't know what it is."

"One of the most deadly diseases of warm-blooded animals. Spreads like wildfire when it gets a start. It can infect human beings, too. How could it happen here? There hasn't been a case of anthrax in the valley for years!"

"I remember Dave Whitaker saying his uncle got two new horses from a farmer near Britton just a week before the comet," said Ken. "Maybe it could have come from there."

"Perhaps," said Smithers.

"What can we do?" asked Professor Maddox. "Can't we start a program of vaccination to keep it from spreading?"

"How much anthrax vaccine do you suppose there is in the whole town? Before we decide anything I want to get Hart and make some tests. If he agrees with me we've got to get hold of the Mayor and the Council and decide on a course of action tonight."

Hart was the other veterinarian, a younger man, inclined to look askance at Dr. Smithers' older techniques.

"I'd just as soon take your word," said Professor Maddox. "If you think we ought to take action, let's do it."

"I want Hart here first," said Smithers. "He's a know-it-all, but he's got a good head and good training in spite of it. Someday he'll be a good man, and you'll need one after I'm gone."

"I'll go," said Ken. "You've already been out, Dad. It's only 4 or 5 blocks, and I feel fine."

"Well, if you feel strong enough," said his father hesitantly. Fatigue was obvious in his face.

Dr. Hart was asleep when Ken pounded on his door. He persisted until the veterinarian came, sleepily and rebelliously. Ken told his story quickly.

Hart grunted in a surly voice. "Anthrax! That fool Smithers probably wouldn't know a case of anthrax if it stared him in the face. Tell him to give your horse a shot of terramycin, and I'll come around in the morning. If I went out on every scare, I'd never get any sleep."

"Dr. Hart," Ken said quietly. "You know what it means if it is anthrax."

The veterinarian blinked under Ken's accusing stare. "All right," he said finally. "But if Smithers is getting me out on a wild-goose chase I'll run him out of town!"

Smithers and Professor Maddox were still beside the ailing horse when Ken returned with Dr. Hart. No one spoke a word as they came up. Hart went to work on his examination, Ken holding the lantern for him.

"Here's a carbuncle, right back of the ear!" he said accusingly. "Didn't anybody notice this earlier?"

"I'm afraid not," Ken admitted. "I guess I haven't taken very good care of him."

"Ken's been in the hospital," Professor Maddox said.

"I know," Hart answered irritably, "but I think anybody would have noticed this carbuncle; these infections are characteristic. There's not much question about what it is, but we ought to get a smear and make a microscope slide check of it."

"I've got a 1500-power instrument," said Ken. "If that's good enough you can use it."

Hart nodded. "Get some sterile slides."

*   *   *   *   *

Afterward, Smithers said, "We've got to get Jack Nelson first and find out how much anthrax vaccine he's got in his store. Nobody else in town will have any, except maybe some of his customers who may have bought some lately. What about the college laboratories? Do they have any?"

"I don't know," said Professor Maddox. "We'll have to contact Dr. Bintz for that."

"Let's get at it," said Hart. "We've got to wake up the Mayor and the Council. The cattle committee will have to be there. Nelson and Bintz, too. We'll find out how much vaccine we've got and decide what to do with it."

Two hours later the men met in the Council chambers of City Hall. Because of the lack of heat, they retained their overcoats and sheepskin jackets. The incrusted snow on their boots did not even soften. In soberness and shock they listened to Dr. Smithers.

"Nobody grows up in a farming community without knowing what anthrax means," he said. "We've got a total of twenty-eight hundred head of beef and dairy cattle in the valley, plus a couple of thousand sheep, and about a hundred horses.

"Jack Nelson's stock of vaccine, plus what he thinks may be in the hands of his customers, plus some at the college is enough to treat about a thousand animals altogether. Those that aren't treated will have to be slaughtered. If they prove to be uninfected they can be processed for meat storage.

"Some vaccine will have to be held in reserve, but if we don't clean up the valley before next year's calf crop we won't stand a chance of increasing our herds. That's the situation we're up against, Gentlemen."

Mayor Hilliard arose. "The only question seems to me to be which animals are of most worth to us. I say we should let all the sheep go. A cow or a horse is worth more than a sheep to us now.

"That leaves the question of the horses. Which is worth more to us: a horse or a cow? We can't haul logs without horses, but we won't need to worry about staying warm if we haven't got food enough."

Harry Mason of the fuel committee stood up immediately. "I say we've got to keep every horse we've got. It would be crazy to give any of them up. There aren't enough now to haul the fuel we need."

"A horse is a poor trade for a cow in these times," protested the food committee's chief, Paul Remington. "Every cow you let go means milk for two or three families. It means a calf for next year's meat supply. We can freeze and still stay alive. We can't starve and do the same thing. I say, let every horse in the valley go. Keep the cows and beef cattle."

An instant hubbub arose, loudly protesting or approving these two extreme views. Mayor Hilliard pounded on the desk for order. "We've got to look at both sides of the question," he said, when the confusion had died down. "I know there are some horses we can lose without much regret; they don't haul as much as they eat. What Paul says, however, is true: Every horse we keep means trading it for a cow and the food a cow can provide.

"I think we need to keep some horses, but it ought to be the bare minimum. I've got an idea about this log hauling. Right now, and for a long time to come, we don't need horses once the logs are on the road. It's a downgrade all the way to town. When the road freezes hard we can coast a sled all the way if we rig a way to steer and brake it properly. There are only two bad curves coming out of the canyon, and I think we can figure a way to take care of them. Maybe a team at each one.

"This would leave most of the horses free to snake the logs out of the hills to the road. I'm for cutting the horses to twenty-five, selecting the best breeding stock we've got, and including the ones needed for emergency riding, such as the Sheriff has."

For another hour it was argued back and forth, but in the end the Mayor's plan was adopted. Then Dr. Aylesworth, who had not previously spoken during the whole meeting, arose quietly.

"I think there's something we're forgetting, Gentlemen," he said. "Something we've forgotten all along. Now that we are faced with our most serious crisis yet, I suggest that you members of our city government pass a resolution setting aside the next Sabbath as a special day of prayer. Ask the ministers of all our denominations to co-operate in offering special prayer services for the safety of our animals, which we need so badly, and for the success of those who are working on College Hill and elsewhere to find a solution to this grave problem."

Mayor Hilliard nodded approvingly. "We should have done it long ago," he agreed. "If no one has any objections I will so declare as Dr. Aylesworth has suggested." There were nods of approval from everyone in the room.

By dawn the next morning the crews were ready to begin the vaccination program. One by one, they examined the animals to make sure the best were saved. The rest were slaughtered, examined for signs of anthrax, and most were prepared for storage.

*   *   *   *   *

On Sunday, while the cattle crews still worked, Ken and his parents attended services in Dr. Aylesworth's congregation. A solemnity was over the whole valley, and the only sound anywhere seemed to be the tolling of the bells in the churches.

The anthrax outbreak had seemed to the people of Mayfield one more, and perhaps a final, proof that their hope of survival was beyond all realization. Before, with severe rationing, it had seemed that they would need a miracle to get them through the winter. Now, with the brutally lessened supply of milk and breeding cattle, it seemed beyond the power of any miracle.

Dr. Aylesworth's white mane behind the pulpit was like a symbol testifying that they never need give up hope as long as any desire for life was in them. In himself there seemed no doubt of their eventual salvation, and in his sermon he pleaded with them to maintain their strength and hope and faith.

In his prayer he asked, "Father, bless our cattle and our beasts of burden that this illness that has stricken them may be healed. Bless us that our hearts may not fail us in this time of trial, but teach us to bear our burdens that we may give thanks unto Thee when the day of our salvation doth come. Amen."

12
DECONTAMINATION

By late November some drifts of snow on the flats were 3 feet deep. The temperature dropped regularly to ten or more below zero at night and seldom went above freezing in the daytime. The level of the log pile in the woodyard dropped steadily in spite of the concentrated efforts of nearly every available able-bodied man in the community to add to it. Crews cut all night long by the light of gasoline lanterns. The fuel ration had to be lowered to meet their rate of cutting.

The deep snow hampered Mayor Hilliard's plan to sled the logs downhill without use of teams. Criticisms and grumblings at his decision to sacrifice the horses grew swiftly.

There had been no more signs of anthrax, and some were saying the whole program of vaccination and slaughter had been a stupid mistake. In spite of the assurance of the veterinarians that it was the only thing that could have been done, the grumbling went on like a rolling wave as the severity of the winter increased.

The Council was finally forced to issue a conservation order requiring families to double up, two to a house, on the theory that it would be more efficient to heat one house than parts of two. Selection of family pairings was optional. Close friends and relatives moved together wherever possible. Where no selection was made the committee assigned families to live together.

As soon as the order was issued, Ken's mother suggested they invite the Larsens to move in with them. The Swedish family was happy to accept.

Thanksgiving, when it came, was observed in spirit, but scarcely in fact. There were some suggestions that

Mayor Hilliard should order special rations for that day and for Christmas, at least, but he stuck to his ironhard determination that every speck of food would be stretched to the limit. No special allowance would be made for Thanksgiving or any other occasion until the danger was over.

Ken and his father and their friends had done their share of criticizing the Mayor in the past, but they now had only increasing admiration for his determination to take a stand for the principles he knew to be right, no matter how stern. Previously, most of the townspeople had considered him very good at giving highly patriotic Fourth of July speeches, and not much good at anything else. Now, Ken realized, the bombastic little man seemed to have come alive, fully and miraculously alive.

*   *   *   *   *

The day after Thanksgiving Ken and Professor Maddox were greeted by Mrs. Maddox upon coming home. "Maria wants you to come to the radio shack right away," she said. "There's something important coming in from Berkeley."

They hurried to the shack, and Maria looked up in relief as they entered. "I'm so glad you're here!" she cried. "Dr. French is on the radio personally. I've been recording him, but he wants to talk to you. He's breaking in every 10 minutes to give me a chance to let him know if you're here. It's almost time, now."

Ken and his father caught a fragment of a sentence spoken by the Berkeley scientist, and then the operator came on. "Berkeley requesting acknowledgment, Mayfield."

Ken picked up the microphone and answered. "This is Mayfield, Ken Maddox talking. My father is here and will speak with Dr. French."

Professor Maddox sat down at the desk. "This is Professor Maddox," he said. "I came in time to hear your last sentence, Dr. French. They tell me you have something important to discuss. Please go ahead."

Ken switched over to receive, and in a moment the calm, persuasive voice of Dr. French was heard in the speaker. "I'm glad you came in, Dr. Maddox," he said. "On the tape you have my report of some experiments we have run the last few days. They are not finished, and if circumstances were normal I would certainly not report a piece of work in this stage.

"I feel optimistic, however, that we are on the verge of a substantial breakthrough in regard to the precipitant we are looking for. I would like you to repeat the work I have reported and go on from there, using your own ideas. I wanted you to have it, along with the people in Pasadena, in case anything should happen here. In my opinion it could be only a matter of days until we have a solution."

"I certainly hope you are right," said Professor Maddox. "Why do you speak of the possibility of something happening. Is there trouble?"

"Yes. Rioting has broken out repeatedly in the entire Bay Area during the past 3 days. Food supplies are almost non-existent. At the university here, those of us remaining have our families housed in classrooms. We have some small stock of food, but it's not enough for an indefinite stay. The rioting may sweep over us. The lack of food may drive us out before we can finish. You are in a better position there for survival purposes. I hope nothing happens to interrupt your work.

"Our local government is crumbling fast. They have attempted to supply the community with seafood, but there are not enough sailing vessels. Perhaps two-thirds of the population have migrated. Some have returned. Thousands have died. I feel our time is limited. Give my report your careful attention and let me know your opinion tomorrow."

They broke contact, uneasiness filling the hearts of Dr. French's listeners in Mayfield. Up to now, the Berkeley scientist had seemed impassive and utterly objective. Now, to hear him speak of his own personal disaster, induced in them some of his own premonition of collapse.

When Maria had typed the report Professor Maddox stayed up until the early-morning hours, studying it, developing equations, and making calculations of his own. Ken stayed with him, trying to follow the abstruse work, and follow his father's too-brief explanations.

When he finished, Professor Maddox was enthusiastic. "I believe he's on the right track," he said. "Unfortunately, he hasn't told all he knows in this report. He must have been too excited about the work. Ordinarily, he leaves nothing out, but he's omitted three or four important steps near the end. I'll have to ask him to fill them in before we can do very much with his processes."

The report was read and discussed at the college laboratory the next day, and the scientists began preliminary work to duplicate Dr. French's results. Ken and his father hurried home early in order to meet the afternoon schedule with Berkeley and get Dr. French to the microphone to answer the questions he had neglected to consider.

As they arrived at the radio shack and opened the door they found Maria inside, with her head upon the desk. Deep sobs shook her body. The receiver was on, but only the crackle of static came from it. The filaments of the transmitter tubes were lit, but the antenna switch was open. The tape recorder was still running.

Professor Maddox grasped Maria by the shoulders and drew her back in the chair. "What is the matter?" he exclaimed. "Why are you crying, Maria?"

"It's all over," she said. "There's nothing more down there. Just nothing..."

"What do you mean?" Ken cried.

"It's on the tape. You can hear it for yourself."

Ken quickly reversed the tape and turned it to play. In a moment the familiar voice of their Berkeley friend was heard. "I'm glad you're early," it said. "There isn't much time today. The thing Dr. French feared has happened.

"Half the Bay Area is in flames. On the campus here, the administration building is gone. They tried to blow up the science building. It's burning pretty fast in the other wing. I'm on the third floor. Did I ever tell you I moved my stuff over here to be close to the lab?

"There must be a mob of a hundred thousand out there in the streets. Or rather, several hundred mobs that add up to that many. None of them know where they're going. It's like a monster with a thousand separate heads cut loose to thrash about before it dies. I see groups of fifty or a hundred running through the streets burning and smashing things. Sometimes they meet another group coming from the opposite direction. Then they fight until the majority of one group is dead, and the others have run away.

"The scientists were having a meeting here until an hour ago. They gathered what papers and notes they could and agreed that each would try to make his own way, with his family, out of the city. They agreed to try to meet in Salinas 6 weeks from now, if possible. I don't think any of them will ever meet again."

A sudden tenseness surged into the operator's voice. "I can see him down there!" he cried in despair. "Dr. French—he's running across the campus with a load of books and a case of his papers and they're trying to get him. He's on the brow of a little hill and the mob is down below. They're laughing at him and shooting. They almost look like college students. He's down—they got him."

A choking sob caught the operator's voice. "That's all there is," he said. "I hope you can do something with the information Dr. French gave you yesterday. Berkeley is finished. I'm going to try to get out of here myself now. I don't think I stand much of a chance. The mobs are swarming all over the campus. I can hear the fire on the other side of the building. Maybe I won't even make it outside. Tell the Professor and Ken so long. I sure wish I could have made it to Mayfield to see what goes with that Swedish accent. 73 YL."

*   *   *   *   *

After dinner, Professor Maddox announced his intention of going back to the laboratory. Mrs. Maddox protested vigorously.

"I couldn't sleep even if I went to bed," he said, "thinking about what's happened today in Berkeley."

"What if a thing like that happened here?" Mrs. Larsen asked with concern. "*Could* it?"

"We're in a much better position than the metropolitan areas," said Professor Maddox. "I think we'll manage if we can keep our people from getting panicky. It's easier, too, because there aren't so many of us."

Professor Larsen went back to the laboratory with the Maddoxes. Throughout the night they reviewed the work of Dr. French. To Ken it seemed that they were using material out of the past, since all of those responsible for it were probably dead.

"We'll have to fill in these missing steps," said Professor Maddox. "We know what he started with and we know the end results at which he was aiming. I think we can fill the gaps."

"I agree," said Professor Larsen. "I think we should not neglect to pass this to our people in Stockholm. You will see that is done?" he asked Ken.

"Our next schedule in that area is day after tomorrow. Or I could get it to them on the emergency watch tomorrow afternoon."

"Use emergency measures. I think it is of utmost importance that they have this quickly."

* * * * *

As the days passed, strangers were appearing more and more frequently in Mayfield. Ken saw them on the streets as he went to the warehouse for his family's food ration. He did not know everyone who lived in the valley, of course, but he was sure some of the people he was meeting now were total strangers, and there seemed so many of them.

He had heard stories of how some of them had come, one by one, or in small groups of a family or two. They had made their way from cities to the north or the south, along the highway that passed through the valley. They had come in rags, half-starved, out of the blizzards to the unexpected sanctuary of a town that still retained a vestige of civilization.

Unexpectedly, Ken found this very subject was being discussed in the ration lines when he reached the warehouse. People had in their hands copies of the twice-weekly mimeographed newssheet put out by the Council. Across the top in capital letters was the word: PROCLAMATION.

Ken borrowed a sheet and read, "According to the latest count we've made through the ration roll, there are now present in Mayfield almost three thousand people who are refugees from other areas and have come in since the beginning of the disaster.

"As great as our humanitarian feelings are, and although we should like to be able to relieve the suffering of the whole world, if it were in our power to do so, it is obviously impossible. Our food supplies are at mere subsistence level now. Before next season's crops are in, it may be necessary to reduce them still further.

"In view of this fact, the Mayor and the City Council have determined to issue a proclamation as of this date that every citizen of Mayfield will be registered and numbered and no rations will be issued except by proper identification and number. It is hereby ordered that no one hereafter shall permit the entrance of any stranger who was not a resident of Mayfield prior to this date.

"A barbed-wire inclosure is to be constructed around the entire residential and business district, and armed guards will be posted against all refugees who may attempt to enter. Crews will be assigned to the erection of the fence, and guard duty will be rotated among the male citizens."

Ken passed the sheet back to his neighbor. His mind felt numb as he thought of some of those he had seen shuffling through the deep snow in town. He knew now how he had known they were strangers. Their pinched, haunted faces showed the evidence of more privation and hardship than any in Mayfield had yet known. These were the ones who would be turned away from now on.

Ken heard the angry buzz of comments all around him. "Should have done it long ago," a plump woman somewhere behind him was saying. "What right have they got to come in and eat our food?"

A man at the head of the line was saying, "They ought to round them all up and make them move on. Three thousand—that would keep the people who've got a right here going a long time."

Someone else, not quite so angry, said, "They're people just like us. You know what the Bible says about that. We ought to share as long as we can."

"Yeah, and pretty soon there won't be anything for anybody to share!"

"That may be true, but it's what we're supposed to do. It's what we've *got* to do if we're going to stay human. I'll take anybody into my house who knocks on my door."

"When you see your kids crying for food you can't give them you'll change your tune!"

Just ahead of him in line Ken saw a small, silent woman who looked about with darting glances of fear. She was trembling with fright as much as with the cold that penetrated her thin, ragged, cloth coat.

She was one of them, Ken thought. She was one who had come from the outside. He wondered which of the loud-mouthed ones beside him would be willing to be the first to take her beyond the bounds of Mayfield and force her to move on.

* * * * *

That night, at dinner, he spoke of it to his parents and the Larsens.

"It's a problem that has to be faced," said Professor Maddox, "and Hilliard is choosing the solution he thinks is right. He's no more heartless than Dr. Aylesworth, for example."

"It seems a horrible thing," said Mrs. Larsen. "What will happen to those who are turned away?"

"They will die," said Dr. Larsen. "They will go away and wander in the snow until they die."

"Why should we have any more right to live than they?" asked Mrs. Maddox. "How can we go on eating and being comfortable while they are out there?"

"*They* are out there in the whole world," said Dr. Larsen as if meditating. "There must be thirty million who have died in the United States alone since this began. Another hundred million will die this winter. The proportion will be the same in the rest of the world. Should we be thankful for our preservation so far, or should we voluntarily join them in death?"

"This is different," said Mrs. Maddox. "It's those who come and beg for our help who will be on our consciences if we do this thing."

"The whole world would come if it knew we had stores of food here–if it could come. As brutal as it is, the Mayor has taken the only feasible course open to him."

Ken and Maria remained silent, both feeling the horror of the proposal and its inevitability.

In the following days Ken was especially glad to be able to bury himself in the problems at the laboratory. His father, too, seemed to work with increasing fury as they got further into an investigation of the material originated by Dr. French. As if seized by some fanatic compulsion, unable to stop, Professor Maddox spent from 18 to 20 hours of every day at his desk and laboratory bench.

Ken stayed with him although he could not match his father's great energy. He often caught snatches of sleep while his father worked on. Then, one morning, as an especially long series of complex tests came to an end at 3 a.m., he said to Ken in quiet exultation, "We can decontaminate now, if nothing else. That's the thing that French had found. Whether we can ever put it into the atmosphere is another matter, but at least we can get our metals clean."

Excited, Ken leaned over the notebook while his father described the results of the reaction. He studied the photographs, taken with the electron microscope, of a piece of steel before and after treatment with a compound developed by his father.

Ken said slowly, in a voice full of emotion. "French didn't do this, Dad."

"Most of it. I finished it up from where he left off."

"No. He wasn't even on the same track. You've gone in an entirely different direction from the one his research led to. *You* are the one who has developed a means of cleaning the dust out of metals."

Professor Maddox looked away. "You give me too much credit, Son."

Ken continued to look at his father, at the thick notebook whose scrawled symbols told the story. So this is the way it happens, he thought. You don't set out to be a great scientist at all. If you can put all other things out of your mind, if you can be absorbed with your whole mind and soul in a problem that seems important enough, even though the world is collapsing about your head; then, if you are clever enough and persevering enough, you may find yourself a great scientist without ever having tried.

"I don't think I'll ever be what the world calls a great scientist," Professor Maddox had said on that day that seemed so long ago. "I'm not clever enough; I don't think fast enough. I can teach the fundamentals of chemistry, and maybe some of those I teach will be great someday."

So he had gone along, Ken thought, and by applying his own rules he had achieved greatness. "I think you give me far too much credit, Son," he said in a tired voice.

13
STAY OUT OF TOWN!

It took a surprisingly short time to ring Mayfield with a barbed-wire barricade. A large stock of steel fence posts was on hand in the local farm supply stores, and these could be driven rapidly even in the frozen ground. There was plenty of wire. What more was needed, both of wire and posts, was taken from adjacent farmland fences, and by the end of the week following the Mayor's pronouncement the task was completed and the guards were at their posts.

In all that time there had been no occasion to turn anyone away, but sentiment both for and against the program was heavy and bitter within the community.

On the Sunday after completion of the fence, Dr. Aylesworth chose to speak of it in his sermon. He had advertised that he would do so. The church was not only packed, but large numbers of people stood outside in the freezing weather listening through the doors. Even greater excitement was stirred by the whispered information that Mayor Hilliard was sitting in the center of the congregation.

The minister had titled his sermon, "My Brother's Keeper." He opened by saying, "Am I my brother's keeper? We know the answer to that question, my friends. For all the thousands of years that man has been struggling upward he has been developing the answer to that question. We know it, even though we may not always abide by it.

"We know who our brothers are—all mankind, whether in Asia or in Europe or next door to our own home. These are our brothers."

As he elaborated on the theme, Ken thought that this was his mother's belief which she had expressed when the fence was first mentioned.

"We cannot help those in distant lands," said Dr. Aylesworth. "As much as our hearts go out to them and are touched with compassion at their plight, we can do nothing for them. For those on our own doorstep, however, it is a different matter.

"We are being told now by our civil authorities in this community that we must drive away at the point of a gun any who come holding out their hands for succor and shelter. We are told we must drive them away to certain death.

"I tell you if we do this thing, no matter what the outcome of our present condition, we shall never be able to look one another in the eye. We shall never be able to look at our own image without remembering those whom we turned away when they came to us for help. I call upon you to petition our civil authorities to remove this brutal and inhumane restriction in order that we may be able to behave as the civilized men and women we think we have become. Although faced with disaster, we are not yet without a voice in our own actions, and those who have made this unholy ruling can be persuaded to relent if the voices of the people are loud enough!"

He sat down amid a buzz of whispered comment. Then all eyes turned suddenly at the sound of a new voice in the hall. Mayor Hilliard was on his feet and striding purposefully toward the pulpit.

"Reverend, you've had your say, and now I think I've got a right to have mine. I know this is your bailiwick and you can ask me to leave if you want to. However, these are my people six days a week to your one. Will you let me say my piece?"

Dr. Aylesworth rose again, a smile of welcome on his face. "I think we share the people, or, rather, they share us on all 7 days of the week," he said. "I will be happy to have you use this pulpit to deliver any message you may care to."

"Thanks," said Mayor Hilliard as he mounted the platform and stood behind the pulpit. "Dr. Aylesworth and I," he began, "have been good friends for a long time. We usually see eye to eye on most things, but in this we are dead opposite.

"What he says is true enough. If enough of you want to protest what I've done you can have a change, but that change will have to include a new mayor and a new set of councilmen. I was elected, and the Council was elected to make rules and regulations for the welfare of this community as long as we were in office.

"We've made this rule about allowing no more refugees in Mayfield and it's going to stand as long as we're in office. By next summer, if the harvest is even a few days late, your children are going to be standing around crying for food you can't give them, and you are going to have to cut your supplies to one-fifth their normal size. That's the way it adds up after we count all the people in the valley, and all the cases and sacks of food in the warehouses.

"It's just plain arithmetic. If we keep adding more people we're all going to get closer and closer to starvation, and finally wake up one morning and find we've gone over the edge of it.

"Now, if that's what you want, just go ahead and get some city officers who will arrange it for you. If anybody in this town, including you, Dr. Aylesworth, can think of a more workable answer or one that makes better sense than the one we've got I'd like to know about it."

It snowed heavily that afternoon out of a bitter, leaden sky. It started in the midst of the morning service, and by the time the congregation dispersed it was difficult to see a block away.

There was little comment about what they had heard, among the people leaving the church. They walked with heads bowed against the snow toward their cold homes and sparsely filled pantries.

The community chapel was near the edge of town. One of the boundary fences lay only two blocks away. From that direction, as the crowd dispersed, there came the sudden sound of a shot. It was muffled under the heavy skies and the dense snow, but there was no mistaking the sound.

Ken jerked his head sharply. "That must have been one of the guards!" he said. His father nodded. Together, they raced in the direction of the sound. Others began running, too, their hearts pounding in anticipation of some crisis that might settle the unanswered questions.

Ken noticed ahead of them, through the veil of snow, the chunky figure of Mayor Hilliard running as rapidly as he could. As they came to the fence they saw the guard standing on one side, his rifle lowered and ready. On the other side of the barbed-wire enclosure was a stout, middle-aged man. He wore an overcoat, but there was no hat on his head. His face was drawn with agony and uncomprehending despair.

He staggered on his feet as he pleaded in a tired voice. "You've got to let me come in. I've walked all the way in this blizzard. I haven't had any food for two days."

A group of churchgoers lined the fence now, additional ones coming up slowly, almost reluctantly, but knowing they had to witness what was about to take place. Ken exclaimed hoarsely to his father, "That's Sam Baker! He runs the drugstore and newsstand in Frederick. Everybody in Mayfield knows Sam Baker!"

Sam Baker turned in bewildered, helpless pleading to the crowd lined on the other side of the fence. Mayor Hilliard stood back a dozen yards from the wire.

"You've got to help me," Sam Baker begged. "You can't make me go back all that way. It's 50 miles. There's nothing there. They're all dead or lost in the snow. Give me something to eat, please..."

"You've got to move on," the guard said mechanically. "Nobody gets in. That's the law here."

Along the fence, people pressed close, and one or two men started hesitantly to climb. Mayor Hilliard's voice rang out, "Anybody who goes on the other side of that fence *stays* on the other side!"

The men climbed down. No one said anything. Sam Baker scanned them with his helpless glance once more. Then he turned slowly. Fifty feet from the fence he fell in the snow, face down.

Mayor Hilliard spoke slowly and clearly once more. "If anyone so much as throws a crust of bread over that fence the guard has orders to shoot."

As if frozen, the onlookers remained immobile. The guard held his fixed stance. Mayor Hilliard stood, feet apart, his hands in his pockets, staring defiantly. On the other side of the fence, the thick flakes of snow were rapidly covering the inert form of Sam Baker. In only a few moments he would be obliterated from their sight. That would be the signal for them all to turn and go home, Ken thought.

Impulsively, he took a step forward. He looked at his father's face. "Dad..."

Professor Maddox touched Ken's arm with a restraining hand. His face was grim and churned by conflicting desires.

The utter stillness was broken then by the crunching sound of boots in the snow. All eyes turned to the powerful, white-maned figure that approached. Dr. Aylesworth was hatless and the snow was thick in his hair. He paused a moment, comprehending the situation. Then he strode forward to the fence.

He put a foot on the wire, and climbed. His coat caught on the barbs as he jumped to the other side. He ripped it free, ignoring the tear of the fabric.

Mayor Hilliard watched as if hypnotized. He jerked himself, finally, out of his immobility. "Parson!" he cried. "Come back here!"

Dr. Aylesworth ignored the command. He strode forward with unwavering steps.

"It's no different with you than it is with any other man," Hilliard shouted. He took the gun from the guard. "You're breaking the law. If you don't stop I'll shoot!"

The majestic figure of the minister turned. He faced Hilliard without hesitation. "Shoot," he said. He turned back and moved once more to the fallen druggist.

There was sweat on Mayor Hilliard's face now. He brushed it with a gloved hand. His hat fell unnoticed to the ground. He raised the gun no higher. "Aylesworth," he called, and his voice was pleading now, "we've got to do what's right!"

The minister's voice came back to him, hollowly, as if from an immense distance. "Yes, we've got to do what's right." Dr. Aylesworth could be seen faintly through the veil of snow as he bent down, raising the druggist's heavy form to his own back in a fireman's carry, then turning to retrace his steps.

Mayor Hilliard let the gun sag in his hands. At the fence Dr. Aylesworth paused. "Separate those wires," he ordered those standing near.

They hastily obeyed, pressing their feet on the lower wire, raising the center one. "Take him!" the minister commanded. He rolled the figure of Sam Baker gently through the opening and crawled through himself. "Bring him to my house," he said. Without a glance at the Mayor, he strode off through the parted crowd and disappeared.

One by one, the onlookers followed, slowly, never glancing at the immobile figure of the Mayor. Hilliard watched the last of them fade into the snow curtain, and he stood there alone, still holding the gun in his hand.

The guard came up at last. "Do you want me to keep on here, Mr. Hilliard?"

*   *   *   *   *

"I still say it was the only thing to do," said Mrs. Maddox at the dinner table. "How could anyone claim to be human and think of leaving poor Mr. Baker lying there in the snow?"

"It was the only thing Dr. Aylesworth could do," said Professor Maddox. "Mayor Hilliard did the only thing *he* could do. Which was right, and which was wrong–I don't think any of us are really sure any more."

"What do you suppose may come of this?" asked Professor Larsen.

"I don't know," Ken's father admitted. "There's a lot of excitement in town. A fellow named Meggs is stirring up talk against Hilliard. He's the storekeeper who tried to hold a profiteering sale, you remember."

"I heard there were some fights in town after church," said Maria.

Ken nodded. "Yes, I heard about them, too."

"It mustn't start here!" exclaimed Mrs. Larsen. "That must be the way it began in Chicago and Berkeley. We can't let it happen here!"

*   *   *   *   *

During the next few days a kind of unspoken truce seemed to reign over the town. It was rumored that both Mayor Hilliard and Dr. Aylesworth were waiting for the other to come for a talk, but that neither was willing to go first under the circumstances. Orders had been given that Sam Baker was to get no special ration. He would get only what others shared with him out of their own meager allotment.

In the laboratory on College Hill it was confirmed that Professor Maddox had indeed discovered a completely effective means of cleansing metals of the destroying dust. Art Matthews and the science club boys were once again scouring the town for engine parts that could be cleaned and used in assembling new and, this time, workable engines.

On Friday morning Professor Douglas came in late, after all the others had been there for a couple of hours. He was panting from his rapid walk up the hill. "Have you heard the news?" he exclaimed.

The others looked up. "What news?" Professor Maddox asked.

"A couple of farmers and ranchers from the south end of the valley rode in about 3 o'clock this morning. They were half-dead. They said their places and several others had been attacked last night. Everything in the whole southern part of the valley, beyond the point, has been looted and burned. Six families, still living on their own places were wiped out."

"Who did it?" Professor Larsen exclaimed.

"Nomads! The ranchers say there's a band of over three thousand camped down by Turnerville, about 20 miles from here. They've been moving across the country, killing and looting everything that's in their way. Now they're headed for Mayfield. They've heard about us having a big cache of supplies."

All work in the laboratory ceased as the men gathered around Professor Douglas. They stared into the distance, but their thoughts were alike.

"Three thousand," said Professor Maddox slowly. "We could put twice that many good men against them. We ought to be able to stand them off, if they attack. What's Hilliard doing about it?"

"He wants us all down there this morning. There doesn't seem to be much question about him staying on as Mayor since this came up."

In a group the men left the half-completed experiments and made their way down the hill to the City Hall. When they arrived they found the Council chamber already filled. The Mayor and the councilmen were at their conference table on the platform in front of the room.

At one side, facing both the leaders and the audience, were three ragged, unshaven strangers in heavy boots and ill-fitting coats. They had not bothered to remove the fur-lined caps from their heads.

Nomads, Ken thought. It was apparent what was going on.

"We're coming in," the center man was saying. His massive size and strength showed even under the thick covering of clothes. "I say we're coming in, and we either come peaceable and you treat us right or we come in our own way. It doesn't make much difference to us how we do it. You just call the shots, Mister, and we'll play it your way. We've got two thousand armed men who know how to shoot fast and straight because they've done a lot of it the last two months. They're the ones that shot faster and straighter than the guys they were shooting at."

"You want to live here peaceably with us, is that it?" questioned Mayor Hilliard.

The man laughed harshly. "Why sure! We're peaceful people, aren't we, Men?" He took reassurance from his grinning companions. "Just as peaceful as them around us."

"How about those ranch families you murdered last night?"

The speaker laughed again. "They didn't want peace, did they, Men? All we asked for was a little something to eat and they started an argument with us. We just don't like arguments."

Mayor Hilliard glanced beyond the table to the first row of listeners. His glance fell upon Dr. Aylesworth. "Before giving my consent to your coming in," he said slowly, "I'd like to hear from one of our more prominent citizens. This is Dr. Aylesworth, one of our ministers. Would you like to tell these people how we feel about their proposal, Reverend?"

The minister rose slowly, his eyes never leaving the three nomads. "It will be a pleasure to tell them." Then to the three he said, "You can go right back where you came from. That's our answer to your proposal."

The big man snarled. "So that's the way you want it, is it? Well then, we'll be back, and when we come you'll wish you'd sung a different tune!"

Mayor Hilliard smiled a wry smile. "I didn't expect our minister to be quite so unfeeling of your plight. Since I am in agreement with his views, however, I must say that you will not be back, because you are not going anywhere. Sheriff, arrest these men!"

Instantly, the big man dropped his hand to his pocket. Before his gun was halfway out, a shot rang from the rear doorway of the crowded room. The stranger dropped to the platform like a crumpled bull.

"You're covered," said Hilliard to the other two. "You came here with a white flag, but it had our people's blood all over it. We are not violating any truce because this is not an affair of honor among gentlemen. It's going to be only an extermination of wild beasts!"

14
MOBILIZATION

The two nomads stood glaring and snarling before the drawn revolvers that pointed at them from the doorways of the room. For an instant it looked as if they were going to draw their own weapons and make a pitched battle of it right there in the Council chamber. Then their glances fell on their comrade, writhing in pain on the floor. They raised their hands in slow surrender.

"If we're not back by sundown, you'll be wiped out!"

"When will the attack begin if you do go back?" asked Hilliard bitterly. "Two hours before sundown? We thank you for the information about your timetable, at least. We have 3 hours to prepare a defense of the town." He nodded to the policeman. "Take them away. Put them in cells and tie them up until this is over."

When they had been removed he turned back to the group. "I've had nightmares," he said, "and this has been one of them. I guess if I had been the Mayor some people think I ought to have been, we would have been drilling and rehearsing our defenses for weeks. I had planned to do so soon. I thought we'd have more time; that's my only excuse.

"The Sheriff and I have done a little preliminary planning and thinking. We've made an estimate of weapons available. From what Jack Nelson and Dan Sims report on hunting licenses issued locally a year ago, there must be about two thousand deer rifles in town. They also guess about four or five hundred 22's. We're lucky to live in hunting country.

"Dan and Jack have about two hundred guns of all kinds and sizes in their rental and selling stock, and they've got nearly all the ammunition in the valley. They had stocked up for the hunting season, which we never had this year, so their supply sounds as if it would be pretty good. You've got to remember the difference in requirements for bagging a deer and carrying on a war. We have very little ammunition when you consider it from that angle.

"The police, of course, have a few guns and some rounds. I'm placing Sheriff Johnson in full charge of defense. The police officers will act as his lieutenants." The Mayor stepped to a wall chart that showed the detailed topography of Mayfield and its environs. "This is your battle map right here, Sheriff. Come up and start marking off your sectors of the defense perimeter and name your officers to take charge of each. I hope somebody is going to say it's a good thing we've got the barbed-wire defense line before this meeting is over!

"I want a rider to leave at once to bring back the wood detail. All their horses will be turned over to the police officers for use in their commands. I want fifty runners to go through town and notify one man in each block to mobilize his neighbors, with all weapons available, and lead them to the sectors which the Sheriff will designate. Each man will bring all the ammunition he owns. Additional stores will be distributed by wagon to the sectors. Above everything else, each man must be warned to make each shot count."

The room was silent, and there was no protest or disagreement. Mayor Hilliard, the man who had made fancy speeches, seemed to have vanished. Hilliard, the dynamic, down-to-earth leader had taken his place. For a moment no one in the room was more surprised than Hilliard himself.

"There's one thing I want to make absolutely clear," he said after a pause. "You people who are working at the laboratory on College Hill are to keep away from the front-lines and away from all possible danger. That's an order, you understand?"

"No," said Professor Maddox abruptly. "It's our duty as much as anyone else's to share in the defenses."

"It's your duty to keep your skins whole and get back into the laboratories as quickly as you can and get things running again! We haven't any special desire to save your necks in preference to our own, but in the long run you're the only hope any of us has got. Remember that, and stay out of trouble!"

The Sheriff made his appointments in rapid-fire sequence, naming many who were not present, ordering messengers sent to them. Ken volunteered to ride after the wood detail.

"I guess it's safe enough to let you do that," the Mayor said. "Make it fast, but don't break your neck."

"I'll take it easy," Ken promised.

Outside, he selected the best of the three police horses and headed up out of town, over the brittle snow with its glare ever-reminding of the comet. When he was on higher ground, he glanced back over the length of the valley. The nomads were not in sight. Not in force, anyway. He thought he glimpsed a small movement a mile or two away from the barrier, at the south end of the valley before it turned out of sight at the point, but he wasn't sure. Once he thought he heard a rifle shot, but he wasn't sure of that, either.

As he appeared at the edge of the forest clearing, Mark Wilson, foreman of the detail, frowned irritably and paused in his task of snaking a log out to the road.

"You'll ruin that horse, besides breaking your neck, riding like that in this snow. You're not on detail, anyway."

"Get all your men and horses up here right away," Ken said. "Mayor's orders to get back to town at once." He told briefly the story of what had happened.

Mark Wilson did not hesitate. He raised a whistle to his lips and signaled for the men to cease work and assemble. One by one they began to appear from among the trees. The horses were led along, their dragging harnesses clanking in the frozen air. "We could cut for 2 more hours," they protested. "No use wasting this daylight and having to cut by lantern."

"Never mind," said Wilson. "There's something else to do. Wait for the rest."

When all had assembled he jerked his head toward Ken. "Go ahead," he said. "You tell them."

Ken repeated in detail everything that had happened. He outlined the Mayor's plan of defense and passed on the order for them to take all mounts to City Hall, to go by their own homes on the way and pick up such weapons as they owned. "You'll get your further orders there," he finished.

The group was silent, as if they could not believe it was actually happening. Mark Wilson broke the spell that seemed to be over them. "Come on!" he cried. "Get the lead out of your shoes and let's get down there! Sunset's the deadline!"

There was a rush of motion then. They hitched up the necessary teams and climbed aboard the half-filled sleds. There was no excitement or swearing against fate and their enemies. Rather, a solemn stillness seemed to fill each man as the sleds moved off down the hard, frozen roadway.

Almost, but not quite the same pervading stillness was present in the town when Ken returned. There was a stirring of frantic activity like that of a disturbed anthill, but it was just as silent. The runners moved from block to block. In their wake the alarmed block leaders raced, weapons in hand, from house to house, arousing their neighbors. Many, who had already completed the block mobilization, were moving in ragged formations to the sector ordered by the block runner according to Sheriff Johnson's plan.

Ken did not know what was planned for the many weaponless men who were being assembled. They would be useless at the frontline. There was need for some at the rear. He supposed Johnson would take care of that later when every weapon was manned at the defense barrier.

He stopped at his own house. His mother greeted him anxiously. He could see she had been crying, but she had dried her tears now and was reconciled to the inevitable struggle that was at hand.

"Your father came in a few minutes ago, and left again," she said. "He's been placed in charge of distribution of medical supplies under Dr. Adams. He wants you and the other boys of the club to help in arranging locations for medical care. Meet him at Dr. Adams' office."

"Okay, Mom. How about packing a load of sandwiches? I may not be back for a long time. I don't know what arrangements they are making for feeding the people on duty."

"Of course. I'll make them right away." She hurried to the kitchen.

Maria said, "There must be something I can do. They'll need nurses and aides. I want to go with you."

"I don't know what they've planned in that department, either. They ought to have plenty of room for women in the food and nursing details."

His mother came with the sandwiches and placed them in his hands. "Be careful, Ken." Her voice shook. "Do be careful."

"Sure, Mom."

Maria got her coat. Mrs. Larsen let her go without protest, but the two women watched anxiously as the young people rode toward town on the police horse.

At the doctor's office, Ken found his father surrounded by an orderly whirl of activity. "Ken! I was hoping you'd get back soon. You can help with arrangements for hospital care, in assigned homes. The rest of your friends are out on their streets. Take this set of instructions Dr. Adams has prepared and see that arrangements are made in exact accordance with them at each house on the list."

"I can help, too," said Maria.

"Yes. Dr. Adams has prepared a list of women and girls he wants to assign as nurses and aides. You can help contact them. Get the ones on this list to meet here as quickly as possible and they'll be assigned to the houses which the boys are lining up."

The comet was setting earlier now, so that its unnatural light disappeared almost as soon as the sun set below the horizon. In the short period of twilight, tension grew in the city. Everything possible had been done to mount defenses. An attack had been promised if the nomad emissaries did not return. Now the time had come.

Darkness fell with no sign of activity in any direction. It seemed unreasonable that any kind of night attack would be launched, but Hilliard and Johnson warned their men not to relax their vigilance.

The pace of preparatory activity continued. Blankets, clothing and food were brought to the men who waited along the defense perimeter. Medical arrangements were perfected as much as possible.

Ken and his father made their quarters in another room of the building where Dr. Adams' office was. There was no heat, of course, but they had brought sleeping bags which were unrolled on the floor. After the sandwiches were gone their rations were canned soup, to be eaten directly from the can without being heated.

Maria was quartered elsewhere in the building with some of the women who were directing the nurses' activities.

Through the windows could be seen the campfires which Johnson had permitted to be built at the guard posts. Each had a wall of snow ready to be pushed upon it in case of any sign of attack.

"We'd better get some sleep," Professor Maddox said finally to Ken. "They'll take care of anything that's going to happen out there tonight. We may have a rough day tomorrow."

Ken agreed, although he did not feel like sleeping. After hours, it seemed, of thrashing restlessly he dozed off. He thought it was dawn when he opened his eyes again to the faint, red glow reflected on the walls of the room. He was unaware for a moment of where he was. Then he saw the glow was flickering.

He scrambled to his feet and ran to the window. In the distance the glow of burning houses lit the landscape. The rapid crack of rifle fire came faintly to his ears.

Professor Maddox was beside him. "How could they do it?" Ken exclaimed. "How could they get through our lines and set fire to the houses?"

On the southern sector of the defense line Sheriff Johnson's men crouched behind their improvised defenses. The glow of the fire blinded them as they attempted to pierce the darkness from which the attack was coming.

From a half-dozen different points fireballs were being lobbed out of the darkness. Ineffective on the snow-laden roofs, many others crashed through the windows and rolled on the floors inside. Such targets became flaming infernos within minutes.

They were all unoccupied because the inhabitants had been moved closer to the center of town for protection.

A fusillade of shots poured out of the darkness upon the well-lighted defenders. They answered the fire, shooting at the pinpoints of light that betrayed the enemy's position, and at the spots in the darkness from which the flaming fireballs came. It was obvious that the attackers were continuously moving. It was difficult to know where the launching crews of the fireball catapults were actually located in that overwhelming darkness.

Sheriff Johnson was on the scene almost at once. He had once been an infantry lieutenant with combat experience. His presence boosted the morale of the defenders immediately.

"Hold your fire," he ordered the men. "Keep under cover and wait until you can see something worth shooting at. Try to keep the fire from spreading, and watch for a rush attack. Don't waste ammunition! You'll find yourselves without any if you keep that up."

Reluctantly, they ceased firing and fell back to the protection of their barricades. Patrolman John Sykes, who was lieutenant of the sector, had been in the National Guard, but he had never seen anything like this. "Do you think they'll rush us?" he asked. "Tonight, I mean, in the dark."

"Who knows? They may be crazy enough to try anything. Keep your eyes open."

The flames quickly burned out the interiors of the houses that had been hit. As the roofs crashed in, their burden of snow assisted in putting out the fires, and there was no spreading to nearby houses.

In his room, Ken dressed impatiently. It was useless to try to sleep any more. "I wish they'd let us go out there," he said. "We've got as much right as Johnson or any of the rest."

His father remained a motionless silhouette against the distant firelight. "As much right, perhaps," he said, "but more and different responsibilities. Hilliard is right. If we were knocked down out there who would take over the work in the laboratory? Johnson? Adams?

"In Berkeley there are thousands fighting each other, but with French and his group gone, no one is fighting the comet. I don't think it is selfish to say we are of infinitely more value in the laboratory than we could ever be out there with guns in our hands."

He turned and smiled in the half-darkness. "That's in spite of the fact that you have the merit badge for marksmanship and won the hunting club trophy last year."

After an hour the attack ceased, apparently because the defenders refused to waste their fire on the impossible targets. Sheriff Johnson sent word around for his men to resume rotation of watch and get all the sleep possible before the day that was ahead of them.

The fires burned themselves out shortly before dawn. Their light was followed soon by the glow of the comet rising in the southeast. Ken watched it and thought of Granny Wicks. It wouldn't be hard, he thought, to understand how a belief in omens could arise. It wouldn't be hard at all.

The sky had cleared so that the light of the comet bathed the entire countryside in its full, bitter glory. At sunrise the faint trickles of smoke rose from hundreds of wood fires, started with the difficult green fuel, and stringent breakfasts were prepared. A thought went through Ken's mind and he wondered if anybody was taking note of the supply of matches in town. When they ran low, coals of one fire would have to be kept to light another.

It was 9 o'clock, on a day when ordinarily school bells would have been sounding throughout the valley. The first war shouts of the attacking nomads were heard on the plain to the south. About thirty men on horseback raced single file along the highway that bore the hard, frozen tracks of horses and sleds that had moved to and from the farms down there.

Patrolman Sykes watched them through his glasses. His command rang out to his company. "Hold fire." He knew the nomads would not hope to break through the barbed wire on such a rush. It looked as if they planned an Indian-style attack as the line began breaking in a slow curve something less than 100 yards away.

"Fire!" Sykes commanded. Volleys of shots rang out on both sides almost simultaneously. The lead rider of the nomads went down, his horse galloping in riderless panic at the head of the line. The hard-riding column paralleled the barrier for 200 yards, drawing the fire of adjacent guard posts before they broke and turned south again. It was, evidently, a test of the strength of the defenses.

"Every shot counts!" Sykes cried out to his men. As the attackers rode out of effective range he sighted four riderless horses. Beside him, in the barricade, one of his own men was hit and bleeding badly. A tourniquet was prepared until two men of the medical detail arrived with an improvised stretcher.

Sykes sat down and rested his head on his arms for a moment. The air was well below freezing, but his face was bathed with sweat. How long? he asked himself silently. How long can it go on? First the comet, then this. He roused at a sudden cry beside him.

"They're coming back," a man shouted. Sykes stood up and raised his fieldglasses to his eyes. From around the point a fresh group of riders was pouring toward the town. At least three times as many as before.

In a flash, he understood their intent. "They're going to come through!" he cried. "They're going to come right through the barrier, no matter what it costs them!"

15
BATTLE

The hard-riding nomad cavalry bore down on the defense line. They did not break into a circling column as before, I but began forming an advancing line. When they were 75 yards away, Sykes ordered his men to begin firing.

The nomads were already shooting, and what their emissary had said was true: these men were expert shots, even from horseback. Sykes heard the bullets careening off the sloping face of the barricade. Two of his men were down already.

He leveled his police pistol and fired steadily into the oncoming ranks. He thought they were going to try to jump the fence this time, and he braced for the shock. To his dismay, he now saw that a perfectly clear space for their landing had been left between his own position and the adjacent barricade.

Suddenly the line of attackers swerved to the left just a few feet from the wire. The defending fire was furious, and for a moment Sykes thought they were going to turn the line back. Then several of the nomads raised their arms and hurled dark, small objects toward the barrier. Sykes recognized them even while they were in the air. Grenades.

He shouted to his men and they flattened behind the barricade. Six explosions thundered almost simultaneously. Mud and rocks sprayed into the air and fell back in a furious rain upon the defenders.

Cautiously, Sykes lifted himself from the ground and got a glimpse of the scene once more. A hundred feet of barbed-wire fence had disappeared in a tangle of shattered posts and hanging coils. Through the opening, the nomads poured over the barricades in the midst of Sykes' men. Smashing hoofs landed almost upon him but for his frantic rolling and twisting out of their path. Gunfire was a continuous blasting wave. Sykes thought he heard above it the sound of Johnson's voice roaring commands to the retreating men.

It sounded like he was saying, "Close up! Close up!" but Sykes never knew for sure. An enormous explosion seemed to come from nowhere and thunder directly in front of him. The day darkened suddenly and he felt himself losing all control of his own being. He wondered if a cloud had crossed the sun, but almost at the same time he ceased to be concerned about the question at all.

*   *   *   *   *

The first of the wounded came in slowly, borne by stretcher bearers on foot who had literally dragged their charges through the lines of invading horsemen. Ken directed their assignment to the hospital-houses. He had always believed he could take a scene like this in his stride, but now he felt he must keep moving constantly to keep from becoming violently sick.

Overhead, a pall of smoke surged again, blotting out, partly, the comet's light. More houses had been fired by the invaders. The sound of crackling flames mingled with the thunder of hoofs and the roll of rifle fire.

Surely it wouldn't be possible, Ken thought, for such a charge to succeed unless it were backed by strong infantry. He moved into one of the houses and directed the placement of the severely wounded man brought up now by the bearers. As they left, he looked down at the stained and bloody face. A nurse was already at work cutting away the matted clothing from the wound.

Ken exclaimed loudly before he realized what he was saying. "Mr. Harris! Mr. Harris—you shouldn't have been out there!"

The man opened his eyes slowly against the terrible pain. He smiled in recognition. It was Mr. Harris, the principal of Mayfield High School; the one Ken had attended. He was an old man–at least fifty–much too old to have been at the barricade with a rifle.

"You shouldn't have been out there," Ken repeated.

Mr. Harris seemed to have difficulty in seeing him.

"Ken," he said slowly. "It's Ken Maddox, isn't it? Everybody has to do something. It seemed like this was the best thing I could do. No school to teach. No school for a long time."

His voice wavered as he began to ramble. "I guess that makes all the students happy. No school all winter long. I always dreamed of Mayfield being a school where they would be glad to come, whose opening in the fall would be welcomed and closing in the spring would be regretted. I never got that far, I guess.

"I didn't do a really bad job, did I, Ken? Mayfield is a pretty good school, isn't it?"

"Mayfield is a swell school, Mr. Harris," said Ken. "It'll be the best day ever when Mayfield opens up again."

"Yes ... when school opens again," Mr. Harris said, and then he was still.

The nurse felt his pulse and regretfully drew the sheet up to cover his face. "I'm sorry," she said to Ken.

Blindly, he turned and went out to the porch. Mr. Harris, he thought, the little bald-headed man they'd laughed at so often with schoolboy cruelty. He had wanted to make Mayfield a good school, so students would be glad to attend.

He'd done that–almost. Mayfield *was* a good school.

Ken looked at the rolling clouds of black smoke in the sky. The gunfire seemed less steady now. Suddenly he was running furiously and with all his strength. He turned down Main Street and headed south. He ran until he caught sight of the first nomad he had seen since the events in the Mayor's Council chamber.

The enemy had stopped his horse, rearing high, while he hurled some kind of incendiary through the window of a house. It exploded inside and billows of flame and smoke poured out. A heart-tight pain gripped Ken. He looked wildly about and saw a fragment of brick lying beside a demolished house nearby.

He snatched up the missile and wound up as if pitching one straight over the corner of the plate. The horseman saw the motion of his arm and tried to whirl, but he was too late. The brickbat caught him at the side of the head and he dropped to the snow without a sound. Ken ran forward and caught up the nomad's rifle and ammunition belt. The horse had fled in panic.

Without a backward glance Ken raced on down the street toward the dwindling sound of battle. The invaders were retreating, streaming from all directions toward the break in the barrier, firing steadily as they came. The defenders were trying to block the escape.

Ken dropped behind a barricade next to an older man he didn't know. He searched for an opening and waited for a rider to cross his sights; then he squeezed the trigger and the man fell. When he looked up again the last of the invaders were gone. Only half of those who had come up to the attack were leaving it.

The men around Ken slowly relaxed their terrible tension. From some lying prone there were cries of pain. Those who could stand did so and revealed their drawn faces to one another.

Teams of the medical group began moving again. A horse-drawn wagon was brought up that had been fitted with boards across the sides so that two layers of wounded men could be carried at once.

Ken heard sudden hoofbeats behind and turned. Sheriff Johnson rode up and surveyed the scene. His eye caught Ken's figure standing in the midst of it, rifle in hand, the captured ammunition belt draped over his shoulder.

"You!" White anger was on Johnson's face. "You were ordered to stay out of the frontline!" he thundered. "Any other man would be court-martialed for such disobedience. Get back where you belong and don't show your face in this area again. I'll jail you for the rest of the fighting if you disobey again!"

Half-ashamed, but half only, for his impulsive action, Ken turned and moved down the street.

"Leave that gun here!" the Sheriff commanded harshly.

Ken gave it to the nearest soldier. He took off the ammunition belt and handed it over too, then resumed his course. He should not have done it, he told himself, but he felt better for it. He felt he had paid a little of his debt to Mr. Harris.

When he reached the hospital center he told his father.

"It wasn't a good thing," said Professor Maddox gently, "but maybe it was something that had to be done."

Throughout the day they continued to bring in the wounded and the dead. There seemed to be an incredible number, but the invaders had suffered heavily, too. Half their force had been lost. A dozen fine horses had been captured, which were a considerable prize.

There was speculation as to why the nomads chose to attack in this manner. They had done great damage, it was true, yet the attack had not had a chance of being decisive in spite of their insane persistence.

Hilliard and Johnson held a staff meeting that afternoon while a sharp watch was kept for further attack. They considered that they had done very well so far. The chief worries were the grenades and incendiaries, which the nomads seemed to have in large quantity.

Toward evening, Johnson asked for two volunteers to go out as scouts to try to reach the top of Lincoln's Peak, west of town, to spot the camp of the nomads and scout their activities. A pair of volunteers was chosen from the many who offered. On two of the best of the nomads' horses, they made their way across the frozen plain and up the small ravine leading to the ridge. Observers watched until they were out of sight in the ravine.

It was agreed the two would return by 6 o'clock. At 5 there was the faint sound of gunfire from somewhere in the hills. The scouts did not return at the appointed time. They did not return at all.

Night came, and word spread among the townspeople of the disappearance of the two scouts. Anxiety increased as it became apparent they were under close surveillance by the enemy. Perhaps it was the intention of the nomads to wear them down with a winter-long siege of attack after attack, until they no longer had the ability or strength to fight.

Hilliard and Johnson doubted this. The nomads were far less equipped for such a siege than Mayfield was.

Maria continued to return to the radio shack in the evening to maintain the schedule with the network. She reported the plight of Mayfield to the other stations. From across the country came the fervent best wishes of those who heard her. Wishes were all they could offer.

The scientists were particularly anguished because they considered the Maddox-Larsen group among the most likely to crack the barrier that kept them from conquest of the comet dust. "Our prayers are with you," the Pasadena group said.

They sent a new report and Maria typed it and showed it to Professor Maddox that evening. He scanned it and put the pages in his coat pocket as he glanced out the window toward College Hill.

"It seems like ages," he said. "I wonder if we'll ever get back up there."

The next attack came well before dawn. Sheriff Johnson was among the first to be aware of it. The thunder of seemingly countless horses' hoofs was heard faintly out of the south and he put his glasses to his eyes. The nomads were a black patch against the snow.

"How many horses have they got?" he exclaimed to the patrolman beside him. This was Ernest Parkin, one of his best officers.

"I'd say there must be at least a hundred of them," said Parkin in awe. "They must have been gathering horses for weeks."

"Feed," said Johnson, "for themselves and the animals–they may be rabble and savages, but they've had genius of leadership."

Behind shelter, they waited for the blow. All orders had already been given. Only the general alarm was sounded now. It had been expected that the previous pattern of attack would be repeated. The defenders had been moved back from the barbed wire. They fired slowly and methodically with a splendidly efficient barrage as the nomads swung out of the night to blast with their grenades at the reconstructed fence.

The way opened and they plunged in, the defenders closing behind and retreating to the other side of their barricades.

Ken paced restlessly as he heard the shooting. "I'm going up on the roof," he told his father. "There can't be any objection to that."

"I guess not. I'll call you when we need you."

Ken climbed the stairs of the 6-story building, which was the highest in Mayfield. He came out on the frozen surface of the roof and looked into the distance. The mounted invaders were circling like Indians about several blocks of houses, firing steadily at the defenders and hurling incendiaries at the houses.

Then, as Ken turned his eyes to the northern end of the valley, he felt as if the whole world had suddenly fallen to pieces in the dim, morning light.

On foot, a vast host of the invaders moved toward the northern defenses of the town. Instantly, he understood their strategy. While their small parties of mounted attackers had pressed the southern defenses, giving the impression they intended to make their major approach there, the bulk of their forces had marched entirely around Lincoln's Peak and come upon the northern boundary at night. That was why the peak had been so heavily guarded against the scouts.

It had been a march of over 40 miles to by-pass the valley. Now, however, the nomads were in a position to achieve their goal. The bulk of the town's defense was concentrated in the south. Little stood in the way of the horde advancing from the north.

His heart sickened as he saw them rip through the barbed-wire enclosure. The poorly manned defense posts seemed almost non-existent. Only a scattering of shots was thrown at the invaders.

From somewhere, a warning siren sounded, the agreed-upon signal to indicate invasion in that sector. It was far too late for that, Ken thought. The horde was already in the streets, fanning out, dispersing in the deserted streets.

Ken started for the doorway leading from the roof. His responsibility to College Hill was gone now. Every man in the valley was fighting for his own life. If that battle were lost, College Hill would be only an empty symbol, where ghosts were housed, as in Berkeley, as in Chicago, as in a thousand centers of learning the world around.

With his hand on the latch of the door he paused at a new sound that broke upon the air. An incredible barrage of firing was occurring along northern Main Street near 12th Avenue. He put the fieldglasses to his eyes again and watched the scattering nomads seeking cover. Dozens of them lay where they fell headlong in the streets.

Ken strained his eyes to see where the defense had come from. It was centered in the houses and buildings that lined the streets, and on their rooftops. He could see the ant-sized outlines of figures on those roofs. For a moment he failed to understand. Then he felt a choking sensation in his throat.

In a desperate gamble, Johnson and Hilliard had anticipated this move and prepared for it as best they could. They had allowed the main body of the attackers to enter the town itself and had deployed the majority of their guns to ring them about, while offering only token defense on the south.

This was it. The battle would be fought here and now, in the streets of Mayfield, and before the day was over it would be known whether the city would continue its struggle to live or whether it would become another Berkeley.

16
BLACK VICTORY

The spearhead of the nomad infantry attack broke through between two lightly manned guard posts whose garrisons fled in retreat with a few ineffective shots. The column came through in a widening wedge. As it met more defenders it fell back, but it appeared to the nomads that the whole defense line had crumbled or had been diverted to the south, as anticipated.

They poured along Main Street in the faint dawnlight until they reached 12th Avenue. There, they split and fanned along 12th, east and west. It was their strategy, obviously, to occupy and seal off this large northern sector of the town, which amounted to one-quarter of its total area and cut across a large portion of the business section. They would solidify their position here, destroy all opposition, then move to still another sector until they were in command of the entire town.

It was a strategy that would work, unless everything Mayfield possessed were thrown against it, Ken thought. He saw now why 12th Avenue had been chosen as the line of attack: the defenders were intrenched there and were offering forceful opposition.

He looked for a moment to the south again. The defenses there were light, yet the charge of the mounted nomads had to be contained or they would drive all the way to the center of town, burning and killing as they went. If they succeeded in joining with the infantry they would have split Mayfield's defenses in two.

Johnson had mounted his best men, using the captured nomad horses as well as the town's own. Desperately, this small force was trying to contain and exterminate the fierce-riding enemy. Picked sharpshooters had been carefully stationed with the best rifles available. Although the gunfire was not heavy, Ken could see Johnson's men were taking a heavy toll of the invader.

In the north, the lines of fixed battle had now been established. The nomads had drawn back to positions of cover in the empty houses facing 12th. Their flanks were more mobile, fighting for advantage along streets parallel to Main but some blocks away on either side, and extending all the way back to the point of breakthrough. While he surveyed the scene from the roof, Ken watched the stealthy movement of defenders moving behind the main line to try to surround the enemy. That was the strategy of the defense, and the gamble on which their entire fate hung.

If they succeeded they would have the breach closed, leaving no retreat for the surrounded invader.

The comet slowly appeared, illuminating the scene of battle as if it lay upon some other planet. The day was clear so far, but a band of stratus hung low over the western hills. It would probably be snowing by nightfall, Ken thought.

Through the glasses he recognized the leader of a small patrol that was moving east on 18th Avenue. It was Tom Wiley, the barber. His men were mostly students from the college. They were trying to gain a house farther up the block to provide a covering point from which a general advance of the line on both sides of them could hinge. Tom could not see that an opposing patrol had him under observation.

He led his men into the open to cross the street. Ken wanted to shout for him to go back, but it was impossible to be heard at such distance. The enemy patrol moved out slightly. They centered Tom and his men in a murderous burst of rifle fire. The barber fell. Two of the others were hit, but they managed to reach cover with the rest of their companions.

The body of Tom Wiley lay motionless where it fell in the snow-covered street. Ken could see the sign, just a block away, that read, "Wiley's Barber and Beauty Shop." From where Ken stood, the sign, which jutted out over the sidewalk, seemed to project just above the body of the fallen barber.

Ken hesitated in his resolve to go down there in the midst of the fighting. He thought of Johnson's words and Hilliard's orders. Would the defense strategy succeed? The nomads were trained and toughened by their weeks of fight for survival, but Mayfield's men were only weakened by their strained effort to keep the town alive.

On the eastern side of the encirclement a burst of smoke with a core of orange flame at its center spurted upward from a house. This was followed by a second and a third and a fourth. Defending fighters ran from the rear of the burning houses to the row beyond. Behind the screen of billowing smoke the nomads crept forward to repeat their tactics and fire the houses where the defenders now had cover. It was obvious they recognized the danger of encirclement by forces stronger than any they had anticipated. They were making a desperate effort to straighten their lines parallel to the barbed wire, with their flanks and rear clear of threat.

Ken watched the success of their second incendiary thrust. They could go on indefinitely unless the defenders succeeded in flanking them. That was being attempted now. The defenders moved under the cover of the smokescreen to fire on the advancing nomads. The latter recognized their danger and held to solid cover of houses adjacent to those they had fired.

North of this bulge, however, another column was forming, and Ken saw in sudden horror that it was headed directly toward the warehouse! A house only a half-block from the warehouse burst into flame.

There was a flurry of activity from the defenders as they, too, recognized the fresh danger and brought up reinforcements before the threatened warehouse.

This added resistance seemed to inflame the determination of the nomads. They answered the increased fire sharply. Another incendiary ignited a wooden building a step nearer the warehouse. The defenders tried to flank the threatening column but the latter ran between a row of burning houses along an alleyway, firing additional incendiaries as they went.

Then sudden flame burst against the wooden walls of the old skating rink and licked with red fury along its painted surface. In moments the warehouse was bathed on all sides in seething flame, and the nomad column spread beyond it, unaware of the mortal damage they had done.

*   *   *   *   *

Ken turned away. He walked slowly and decisively down the stairs. He told his father what had just happened. "I'm going out there, Dad," he said. "They're going to wipe us out, or destroy every chance we'll have to survive even if we drive them off. Half of our food supply is gone now. What chance have we got even if we kill every nomad in the valley?"

Ken's father turned to a closet and drew out a .30-06. From a hook he took down a hunter's jacket. Its pockets were loaded with shells, and he had an extra box he gave to Ken.

"Johnson left this here," he said. "He intended it for our use if the nomads reached this far. I think maybe it had better be used before the medical center needs defending."

Ken's eyes lighted with gratefulness. "Thanks, Dad," he said. "I'm glad you're willing."

"I don't know if I'm willing or not. However, I think I agree with you that there's nothing else to be done."

Ken ran from the building, clutching the solid, reassuring weight of the rifle in his hand. His coat pockets and the hunting jacket were weighted heavily with the supply of ammunition. There was a feeling of security in the weapon and the shells, but he knew it was a short-lived, deceptive security.

He went to Eighth Street and turned north, which would bring him close to the burned warehouse. He could see the immense, rolling column of black smoke and hear the bursting crackle of its flames. The whole town could go, he thought, if the fire became hot enough. It would spread from building to building regardless of the snow cover. He glanced at the sky and hoped the snow might soon resume.

From the rooftop, it had seemed to Ken that the small units of the defenders were almost leaderless, and there was lack of co-ordination between them. He came up in their rear ranks and confirmed this suspicion. They seemed to be depending as best they could on unanimous and intuitive agreement about a course of action. What had happened to their sergeants and lieutenants, Ken did not know. Perhaps in their haste of organization there never had been any.

There was top-level command, of course, as appointed by Sheriff Johnson for the entire sector, but it did not extend to the lower levels in any degree Ken could see.

The men paid no attention as Ken joined them. He knew a few of the dozen nearby, but they seemed to regard him as a total stranger. The shock of battle was in their eyes, and they seemed wholly unaware of anything in the world except the desperate necessity to find cover and to destroy the invader.

Ken followed them into the shelter of a house flanking the still-advancing incendiaries. He crouched at a window with an older man whom he did not know and leveled his rifle through an opening. A pair of figures appeared momentarily at the edge of the smoking cloud. The older man jerked his gun and fired frantically and ineffectively.

"Slow!" Ken cried. "Aim before you shoot!"

The man glanced at him in a kind of daze. Ken sighted patiently and carefully. The smoke cloud parted once again and he squeezed the trigger. One of the figures dropped and the smoke cloud closed down again.

Ken's calmness seemed to penetrate his companion who leaned back for a moment to wipe a shaking hand across his sweat-stained face.

"I've never done anything like this before," he murmured helplessly.

"None of us have," said Ken; "but we've got to do it now. Watch it! We're drawing their fire!"

Bullets shattered the window casing above and beside them. Across the room a man crumpled. Ken risked a glance through the window. "We've got to get out!" he exclaimed. "They're going to rush the house!"

It might have been possible to hold if he knew what cover and reinforcements they had in the adjacent houses, but as far as he could tell the small, 12-man patrol might be entirely alone in the area.

Suddenly, it all seemed utterly hopeless without communication, without leadership–how could they hope to withstand?

"Let's go!" he cried. The others seemed willing to follow him. As they went through the back he saw that the next house had indeed been occupied, but they, too, were retreating, not knowing what strength was near.

A new line of defenders was moving up from halfway down the block. Ken held back to shout to the other patrol and to those coming, "Let's stand in the next street!"

There were shouts of assent from down the line and they moved to the shelter of the empty houses.

They were close to the edge of town, near the barbed-wire barricade, and the nomads would obviously make their biggest effort here to wipe out the forces that threatened to close them off. His own group, Ken saw, would also have to make their stand here or risk being pocketed by the uncoiling line of nomads.

"Don't let them get close enough to fire the buildings!" he shouted down the line. The word was passed along with agreement. They broke into small patrols and occupied the houses, Ken joining one that took over the top floor of a 2-story house. This gave them the advantage of good observation, but the added danger of difficult escape in case the house was set on fire. Its walls were brick, however, and offered a good chance of being held.

Within minutes, the nomads had occupied the houses just abandoned. Ken fired rapidly and carefully as he saw them exposed momentarily in their move to new positions. His marksmanship had a telling effect on the enemy, and encouraged his companions. As soon as the nomads had obtained cover however, it was a stalemate.

It was mid-morning already, and Ken wondered how it had grown so late. For an hour or two they exchanged shots with the enemy. Twice, attempts were made to hurl firebombs. Both were driven back.

Beyond this, however, the nomads seemed in no mood to make further attack. They were waiting for darkness, Ken thought, and then they would advance with their firebombs and grenades and have free choice of battle setting. If that happened, Mayfield might be a huge inferno by midnight. They had to seize the initiative from the invaders.

He called his companions and told them how it looked. They agreed. "What can we do?" a tired, middle-aged man asked.

"We've got to take the initiative before they come at us again." Ken glanced at the sky. "Within an hour it may be snowing hard. That will make it more difficult to hit a target. When daylight is almost gone we'll attack them instead of waiting for them to come after us. It can be done if we hit hard and fast enough. We'll lose some men, but not as many as if we wait and let them pick us off with their grenades and incendiaries as they feel like it."

The men considered it dubiously. "We've got a better chance to hit them as they break from cover," someone suggested.

"Not after dark, and that's what they're waiting for. They'll burn our houses and drive us back all night long if we give them the chance. We must not give it to them!"

Reluctant nods of agreement came from his group. "The way you put it, I guess it's the only chance we've got," the former objector agreed.

"I'll talk with the other groups," Ken said.

He moved down the stairs and out the back door of the house. The space between the two houses was entirely open. He flung himself down and crawled. Twice, he heard the whine of bullets above his head.

After heated argument, the group in the next house agreed to the plan to rush the invaders. He moved on down the block, regretting his own lack of authority that made it necessary for him to have to plead for co-operation. He wondered what was happening in the rest of the town. There had been gunfire all day, but it seemed incredible there had been no communication from any other sector or any evidence of command. No one he talked to had any idea what had happened to their command. There had been some in the beginning, but it had simply seemed to vanish. Ken's pleading for co-operation in an attack was the nearest thing to leadership they had seen for hours.

The snow was swirling hard and the sun was almost beyond the hills, what little of it was visible in the clouds. It was getting as dark as he dared allow before giving the signal for attack, but there was one more group to contact. He debated and decided to go to them.

Then, as he entered the rear of the house, he heard the cries of alarm from those houses he had been to. The invaders were breaking out for an incendiary attack.

He seized his gun and fired the signal for their own advance. He ran into the street shouting for the others to follow. The nomads were concentrating their fire charge at the other end of the row of houses, and there the defenders fell back without an attempt to advance.

Like watching a wave turned back by a rocky shore, Ken saw his companions fleeing in disorderly retreat through the rear of the houses to the block beyond. A bullet whizzed by his head. He dropped to the ground and crawled on his stomach to the safety of cover behind a brick house.

For a long time he lay in the snow, unmoving. He could not hold back the sobbing despair that shook him. He had never before known what it was like to be utterly alone. Mayfield was dying and taking away everything that was his own personal world. He had listened to news of the destruction of Chicago and of Berkeley without knowing what it really meant. Now he knew.

For all he knew, the nomads might even now be in control of the major part of the town. He could not know what had happened to his father, to Maria, to anyone.

The crackling of flames in the next house aroused him. He crawled inside the brick house, which was still safe, for a moment of rest. He knew he should be fleeing with the others, but he had to rest.

He heard sporadic shooting. A few nomads were straggling after their companions at the other end of the street. It was too far to shoot. However, one nomad stopped and swung cautiously under the very windows of the burning house next door. Ken leveled his rifle and fired. The bullet caught the man in the shoulder and flung him violently against the wall. Ken saw that he would be buried by the imminent, flaming collapse of that wall.

The man saw it, too. He struggled frantically to move out of the way, but he seemed injured beyond the power to get away.

Ken regarded him in a kind of stupor for a moment. The man out there was responsible for all this, he thought, for the burning and for the killing....

He swung his rifle over his shoulder and went out. Brands were falling upon the wounded enemy. Ken hoisted the man under the arms and dragged him to the opposite side of the adjacent house. The nomad looked at Ken with a strange fury in his eyes.

"You're crazy!" he said painfully. "You're the one who shot me?"

Ken nodded.

"You'll be cut off. Well, it won't matter much anyway. By tomorrow your town will be burned and dead. Soon, we'll all be dead."

Ken kneeled on the ground beside him, as if before some strange object from a foreign land. "What were you?" he asked. "Before, I mean."

The man coughed heavily and blood covered his mouth and thick growth of beard. The bullet must be in his lungs, Ken thought. He helped wipe away the blood and brushed the man's mouth with a handful of snow.

"You're crazy," the nomad said again. "I guess we're all crazy. You're just a kid, aren't you? You want to know what I was a million years ago, before all this?"

"Yes," Ken said.

The man attempted a smile. "Gas station. Wasn't that a crazy thing? No need of gas when all the cars quit. I owned one on the best little corner in Marysvale."

"Why are you with them?" Ken nodded in the darkness toward the distant attackers.

The man glared, twisting with the pain. Then his glance softened. "You'd have done it, too. What else was there? I had a wife, two kids. No food within a hundred miles after we used what was in our own pantry and robbed what we could from the supermarket downtown.

"We all got together and went after some. We got bigger as we went along. We needed men who were good with rifles. We found some. We kept going. People who had food fought to keep it; we fought to take it. That's the way it had to be.

"We heard about your town with its big hoard of food. We decided to get it."

"Did you know you burned half of it this morning?"

"No. That's tough. That's tough all the way around. Don't look at me that way, kid. You would have done the same. We're all the same as you, only we didn't live where there was plenty of food on hand. We were all decent guys before. Me, those guys out in the street that you knocked off. I guess you're decent, too."

"Where's your family now?"

"Twenty miles down the valley, waiting with the rest of the women and children for us to bring them food."

Ken rose slowly to his feet. The man was bleeding heavily from the mouth. His words were growing muffled. "What are you going to do?" he asked.

"Get on with what has to be done," said Ken wearily. He felt sure he must be walking in a nightmare and in just a little while he would awaken. "If there's a chance, I'll try to send somebody after you."

"Never mind me!" the nomad said with sudden fierceness. "I'm done for. You've finished me. If our outfit should be unlucky enough to lose, see my wife and try to do something for my kids. Get some food to them. Tom Doyle's the name," the man said.

A fit of coughing seized him again and blood poured from his mouth. His eyes were closed when he lay back again. "Tom Doyle's the name," his bloody lips murmured. "Don't forget that, kid. Tom Doyle's Service, corner of First and Green in Marysvale. We were all good guys once."

*   *   *   *   *

The snow was so heavy it seemed like a solid substance through which Ken walked. In spite of it, row upon row of houses burned with a fury that lit the whole scene with a glow that was like the comet's own. Above this, the blanket of black smoke lay as if ready to smother the valley as soon as the light was gone.

Ken didn't know for sure where he was going. A kind of aimlessness crept over him and there no longer seemed any rational objective toward which to move. He crept on from house to house in the direction his group had gone, but he could not find any of them. Somewhere he touched the edge of combat again. He had a nightmare of going into a thousand houses, smashing their windows out, thrusting his rifle through for a desperate shot at some fleeing enemy.

The night was held back by a hundred terrible fires. He shot at shadows and ghosts that moved against the flames. He sought the companionship of others who fought, like himself, in a lonely vastness where only the sound of fire and gunshots prevailed.

Later, he moved through the streets stricken with cold that he could not lose even when he passed and stood close to a mass of burning rubble. He had stopped shooting quite a long time ago, and he guessed he was out of bullets. The next time he met someone, he thought, he would ask them to look in his pockets and see if any were left.

He kept walking. He passed streets where the black, charcoal arms of the skeletons of houses raised to the sky. He passed the hot columns of smoke and continued to shiver with cold as they steamed upward to the clouds. He passed others but no one spoke. After a while he threw his gun away because it was too heavy to carry and he was too tired to walk any more.

The falling snow was covering the ruins with a blanket of kind obscurity. Ken kneeled down and was surprised to observe that he wasn't cold any more. He lay full length in the whiteness, cradling his head on his arms, and peace and stillness such as he had never known before closed over him.

*   *   *   *   *

It seemed an eternity later that there was a voice capable of rousing him, a familiar voice calling out in anguish, "Ken, Ken–this is your dad."

He responded, although it was like answering in a dream. "Take care of them, Dad," he said. "Don't let anything happen to them. A woman and two children. Tom Doyle's the name–don't forget that, Tom Doyle."

17
BALANCE OF NATURE

He lay between white sheets, and the stench of burning things was everywhere, in the air that he breathed, in the clean white covers that were over him. His own flesh seemed to smell of it.

He was not quite sure if he were still in a world of dreams or if this were real. It was a golden world; the snow-covered ground beyond the window was gilded with rich, yellow light. He remembered something about such light that was not pleasant. He had forgotten just what it was.

Maria Larsen stood at the foot of his bed. She smiled as his eyes opened. "Hello, Ken," she said. "I've been waiting so long. I've been afraid you'd never wake up."

"Tom Doyle," he said. "Did you find Tom Doyle?"

Maria frowned. "I don't know who you mean!"

"You haven't found his family yet?" Ken cried, struggling to rise in the bed. "Go and find them right now. I promised Tom Doyle I'd do it."

Maria approached and pushed him gently back upon the pillow, drawing the covers over him once more. "Tell me about Tom Doyle," she said. "You've never told me who he is."

It seemed utterly stupid for her not to know, but Ken patiently told her about Doyle's Service, the best little station in the world, at the corner of First and Green. "I told Tom I'd take care of them," he said. "Now go and bring them here!"

"Ken," Maria said, "all the nomads who escaped, and there weren't many, retreated around the south end of town and picked up the women and children they'd left there. They moved on south. That was 3 days ago. We've no idea where they've gone."

Ken tried to rise again against her struggles to hold him down. "They couldn't have gone so far that a man on horseback couldn't find them! Why won't you help me? I promised I'd see to it!"

He lay back weakly, covering his face with his arm. "Go and find Tom Doyle," he said. In detail he described where he had left the man. "You don't believe what I'm saying. Get Tom Doyle and he'll tell you it's the truth."

"He wouldn't be there now. All the wounded, including the nomads, have been moved to homes where they are being cared for. The dead, both theirs and ours, have been burned and their ashes buried."

"Do what I tell you!" Ken implored.

With bewilderment and fear on her face, Maria stood back from the bed and looked at Ken's troubled face. Then quietly she stole from the room and shut the door behind her.

*   *   *   *   *

He had been overworking himself for weeks, Dr. Adams was saying, and had been living on a poor diet that would scarcely keep a medium-sized pup going.

"Then you had a shock, the kind of shock that shakes a man to his very roots. Now you're on your way up again."

Ken glanced about the room. It seemed normal now and there was only a great emptiness within him to replace the frantic urgency he remembered.

"What you're trying to say, Doc, is that I went off my rocker for a while."

Dr. Adams smiled. "If you want to put it that way. However, you're fine now."

Ken stared at the ceiling for a few moments. "Will you still say so if I ask again about Tom Doyle?"

"What do you want to know?"

"Was he found?"

"No. Maria actually tried to find him for you. I'm afraid your Tom Doyle was among the dead."

"I killed him."

"We killed a lot of them—and they killed a lot of our people."

"How did it end?" asked Ken. "I remember the darkness and just wandering around the streets shooting, but I don't know what I hit or where I went."

"That's the way it ended," said Dr. Adams. "House-to-house street fighting, and we won. Don't ask me how. You were in a sector that was cut off almost as soon as you entered it. Even where communication was maintained things were nearly as chaotic.

"Johnson says it was just plain, dumb luck. Hilliard says he doesn't think it really happened. Dr. Aylesworth calls it a miracle, a gift and a blessing that shows we're meant to survive. Most of the rest of us are willing to look at it his way."

"I could do something for Tom Doyle," Ken said finally. "He was a decent guy. They all were, once. I could find his wife and children."

The doctor shook his head. "All who are left of that group of nomads are going to die. We've got to let them die, just as we let the people in Chicago and Berkeley and ten thousand other towns die. We have no more power to save Tom Doyle's family than we had to save them."

"We're taking care of the nomad wounded! We could do as much for just one woman and two kids!"

"We're helping the wounded until they get on their feet," Dr. Adams said quietly. "Then they'll be sent on—to wherever they came from."

Ken stared at him.

"There is only one thing we could never forgive ourselves for," the doctor continued. "That one thing would be letting the Earth itself die. As long as there are people alive who can fight the comet, we still have a chance. Nothing else in the whole world matters now. Don't you see there is no other purpose in keeping Mayfield alive except to support the few people who understand the dust and can fight it? Beyond that, Mayfield has no more right to live than any other town that has already died. But Mayfield has to stay alive to keep you and your father and the others like you fighting the dust."

Dr. Adams gave permission for Ken to be out of bed for a short time. He tried, after the doctor had left, and almost fell on his face. The whole world seemed to spin in enormous cart wheels. He persisted though, and 2 hours later he was making his way slowly up College Hill with the help of Maria who walked beside him and lent her arm for support.

At the top of the hill they stopped and turned for a look at the valley below them. The ruin was plain to see in spite of the snow cover. A third of the town had been completely burned. At the old skating rink, workmen were clawing through the debris for usable remains of food. A miserably small pile of items showed the extent of their success.

Curls of smoke still rose from the ashes, and the nauseating smell of death and burning floated over the whole valley.

Of his own experience Ken felt only a numbing confusion as yet. He thought he should feel like a fool for his collapse at the height of the battle, but he did not. He felt as if he had marched to the absolute edge of human endurance and had looked to the dark pit below.

He turned to Maria. "I'll be okay now. It's time for you to get back to the radio station. Tell them what has happened and get their reports. I'll see you tonight."

It seemed a long time since he had last been in the laboratory. The workers were once more in the midst of their thousands of trials and failures to produce a colloidal, non-poisonous form of the decontaminant, which could be infused in the atmosphere of the world to destroy the comet dust.

He stayed until his father left at 7 o'clock, and they went home together. He still had to depend on someone else for assistance on the steep and slippery hill.

When they reached home Maria had a lengthy report ready from the Pasadena people, and one from Schenectady.

Professor Maddox read the reports at the dinner table. He passed the sheets to Professor Larsen as he finished them. Ken saw he was not reading with his usual thorough analysis. When he had finished he returned to his eating with perfunctory motions.

"Anything new?" Ken asked.

"The same old story. A thousand hours of experiments, and no success. I feel we're all on the wrong track, trying to perfect a chemical colloid, based on the decontaminant, which will destroy the dust. I feel that nothing's going to come of it."

Ken said, "I had a crazy dream the other day while Dr. Adams had me under drugs. I had almost forgotten it. I dreamed I was walking along the street and had a special kind of flashlight in my hand. When I came to a car that wouldn't run, standing by the curb, I turned the beam of the flashlight on it. Then whoever owned it could step in and drive away. After I had done that to all the cars in Mayfield I turned it on the sky and just kept flashing it back and forth and the comet dust fell down like ashes and the air was clean."

Professor Maddox smiled. "A nice dream! I wish we could make it come true. I'm afraid that idea will have to go back to the pages of your science fiction, where it probably came from in the first place."

"Dad, I'm serious!" Ken said earnestly.

"About making a magic flashlight?" His father was almost sarcastic, which revealed the extent of his exhaustion, Ken thought. He was never like that.

"What I'm trying to say is that there are other ways to precipitate colloids. We haven't even given any thought to them. Colloids can be precipitated by heat, by pressure, by vibration. Maybe a dozen other ways that I don't know anything about.

"Maybe some kind of physical means, rather than chemical, is the answer to our problem. Why don't we let Pasadena and the other labs go on with the chemical approach but let us do some work on possible physical means?"

Professor Maddox sat very still. His glance passed from Ken to Professor Larsen. The latter nodded. "I think we have indeed been foolish in ignoring this possibility up to now. I wonder if Ken hasn't got a very good thought there."

"Have you anything specific to suggest?" Ken's father asked.

"Well, I've been wondering about supersonic methods. I know that a supersonic beam can be used for coagulation and precipitation."

"It would depend on the size of the colloidal particles, and on the frequency of the wave, wouldn't it? Perhaps we *could* find a frequency that would precipitate the dust, but I wonder if we wouldn't have the same problem as with mechanical treatment of the Earth's atmosphere. Even if we succeeded on a laboratory scale, how could it be applied on a practical, worldwide scale?"

"I don't know," said Ken. "It may not work out, but I think it's worth trying."

"Yes, I agree. I don't think we'll give up the chemical research, but a group of you can begin work on this supersonic approach tomorrow."

The losses of food at the warehouse were enormous. Less than 5 percent of the contents could be removed in usable form. Most of the canned goods had burst from internal pressure. Grain and other dried products were burned, for the most part. The food supply of the community was now reduced to six-tenths of what it had been.

The population had been reduced by one-tenth, in men killed by the nomads.

Mayor Hilliard and his councilmen struggled to work out a reasonable ration plan, based upon the ratio of supplies to number of consumers. There was no arithmetical magic by which they could stretch the food supply to satisfy minimum needs until next harvest.

There was going to be death by starvation in Mayfield before spring.

Hilliard fought through an agreement in the Council that the researchers on College Hill, and all their families, were to have first priority, and that they were to get full rations at all times in order to keep on with their work.

There were grumblings among the councilmen, but they finally agreed to the wisdom of this. They agreed there were babies and small children who needed a somewhat normal ration, at least. There were over four hundred wounded who had to be cared for as a result of the battle. There were also the aged, like Granny Wicks, and her companions.

"Well try to give the little ones a chance," said Mayor Hilliard, "but the old ones don't need it. Perhaps we can spare a little extra for the wounded who have a chance of survival, but not much. We're going to see that College Hill survives."

Before spring, however, a choice would still have to be made—who was to have the remaining share of food, and who was not?

Privately, Hilliard wondered if any of them had a chance to see another spring.

The decision to support the scientists at the expense of the other inhabitants of Mayfield could not be kept secret. When it became known, a tide of fury swept the community. The general public no longer had any capacity to accept the larger view in preference to relief of their own suffering. One of the college students who worked in the laboratory was beaten by a crowd as he walked through town. He died the same evening.

Suddenly, the scientists felt themselves standing apart, pariahs among their own people. They debated whether to take the allotment. They asked themselves over and over if they were tempted to take it because they shared the same animal greed that gripped the whole town, or if genuine altruism prodded them to accept.

Dr. Adams met their arguments. "You accept," he said, "or everything we fought for is worthless. You can stand the hate of the townspeople. Scientists have done it before, and it's a small sacrifice so long as you can continue your work. Those of us who are supporting you believe in that work. Now get on with it, and let's not have any more of these ridiculous arguments!"

The suggestion of physical means of precipitating the dust came like a burst of light to the entire group as they began to examine the possibilities. Within a week, they had determined there was indeed a broad range of supersonic frequencies capable of precipitating the dust.

The night Professor Maddox and his companions came home to announce their success they were met with the news that Mrs. Larsen was ill. During the day, she had developed a high temperature with severe pains in her body.

Professor Larsen was deeply worried. "She's never been ill like this before."

Ken was sent for Dr. Adams, but the latter did not come for almost 2 hours. When he did arrive, they were shocked by his appearance. His face was lined and hollow with exhaustion, beyond anything they had seen as long as they had known him. He looked as if he were on the verge of illness himself.

He brushed away their personal questions and examined Mrs. Larsen, rather perfunctorily, they thought. However there was no hesitation as he announced his diagnosis. "It's the sixteenth case I've seen today. Over a hundred and fifty this week. We've got an epidemic of flu on our hands. It's no mild, patty-caking kind, either. It's as virulent as any that's ever been experienced!"

Mrs. Maddox uttered a low cry of despair. "How much more must we be called upon to endure?"

No one answered. Dr. Adams rummaged in his bag. "I have vaccine for all of you. I don't know how much good it will do against this brand of bug that's loose now, but we can give it a chance."

"Is everyone in town getting it?" Professor Maddox asked.

Dr. Adams snorted. "Do you think we keep supplies of everything in emergency proportions? College Hill gets it. Nobody else."

"We can't go on taking from everyone else like this!" protested Mrs. Maddox. "They have as much right to it as we. There should be a lottery or something to determine who gets the vaccine."

"Hilliard's orders," said Dr. Adams. "Besides, we've settled all this. You first, Ken."

For a few days after the battle with the nomads, it had seemed as if the common terror had welded all of Mayfield into an impregnable unit. There was a sense of having stood against all that man and nature could offer, and of having won out against it. However, the penetrating reality of impending competition among themselves for the necessities of life, for the very right to live, had begun to shatter the bonds that held the townspeople as one.

The killing of the college student in protest against the partiality to College Hill was the first blast that ripped their unity. Some protested openly against the viciousness of it, but most seemed beyond caring.

There were two events of note in the days following. The first was a spontaneous, almost valley-wide resurgence of memory of Granny Wicks and her warnings. Everything she had said had come true. The feeling swept Mayfield that here in their very midst was an oracle of truth who had been almost wholly ignored. There was nothing they needed to know so much as the outcome of events with respect to themselves and to the town as a whole.

Almost overnight, streams of visitors began to pour toward the home for the aged where Granny lived. When they came, she smiled knowingly and contentedly, as if she had been expecting them, waiting for them. Obligingly, and with the peaceful aura of omniscience, she took them into her parlor and told them of things to come.

At the same time, Frank Meggs felt new stirrings within him. He sensed that he had been utterly and completely right in all his years of criticism of those who managed the affairs of Mayfield. The present condition of things proved it. The town was in utter chaos, its means of survival all but destroyed. Incompetently, its leaders bumbled along, not caring for the mass of the people, bestowing the people's goods on the leaders' favorites. He began saying these things on the streets. He got a box, and used it for a platform, and he shouted from the street corners that the leaders were corrupt, and none of them were safe unless College Hill and City Hall were wiped out. He said that he would be a better mayor than anyone else in Mayfield.

He had listeners. They gathered on the corners in the daytime, and they listened at night by the light of flaming torches. Many people began to believe that he was right.

*   *   *   *   *

A week after Mrs. Larsen's illness, it was evident beyond all doubt that Mayfield was the victim of a killer epidemic. Mayor Hilliard himself was stricken, and he sent word that he wanted Professor Maddox, Ken, and Dr. Larsen to come to his bedside.

He was like a feeble old man when they arrived. All the fire and the life had gone from his eyes, but he brightened a little as they came into the room.

"At least you are still alive," he said gruffly. "I just wanted to make sure of that fact, and I wanted to have a final understanding that it's soaked into your thick heads that nothing is to interfere with your own survival."

"We hope you're not overestimating our worth," said Professor Maddox.

"I don't know whether I am or not! All I know is that if you're not worth saving then nobody is. So, if this town is going to die, you are going to be the last ones left alive, and if you don't give me your word on this right now I'll come back and haunt you every minute you do survive!"

"In order to haunt, you have to be in the proper realm," said Professor Maddox, attempting a joke.

Mayor Hilliard sighed. "I think I can take care of that, too. I'm beat. You're close to it, but you've got to hang on. Carry on with your work on the hill. One thing more: This fellow Meggs has got to be crushed like a worm. When I go, there won't be any election. Johnson is taking over and he'll look out for you, the same as I have done."

"You're going to be all right!" said Professor Maddox. "You'll be up on your feet in another week!"

The Mayor seemed not to have heard him. He was staring at the ceiling, and there was an amused smile at the corners of his lips. "Ain't Mother Nature a funny old gal, though?" he said. "She's planned this to work out just right, and I think it's another of old Doc Aylesworth's signs that Mayfield and College Hill are going to live, so that the rest of the world will, too. It may get knocked pretty flat, but it's going to get up again."

"What are you talking about?" said Ken.

"The invasion of the nomads, and then this flu. Don't you see it? First we get our food supply knocked out, and now old Mamma Nature is going to cut the population down to match it. We tried to figure out who was going to eat and who was going to starve, and now it's going to be all figured out for us.

"Balance of nature, or something, you scientists call it, don't you?" He glanced up at the professors and Ken. "It's a wonderful thing," he said, "just absolutely wonderful!"

18
WITCHCRAFT

Three days later, Mayor Hilliard died. It was on the same day that Maria's mother was buried.

Maria had watched her mother day and night, losing strength and finally lapsing into a coma from which she never emerged.

Maria and her father did their best to control their grief, to see it as only another part of the immense reservoir of grief all about them. When they were alone in their section of the house they gave way to the loss and the loneliness they felt.

There were no burial services. The deaths had mounted to at least a score daily. No coffins were available. Each family dug its own shallow graves in the frozen ground of the cemetery. Sheriff Johnson posted men to help, and to see that graves were at least deep enough to cover the bodies. Beyond this, nothing more could be done. Only Dr. Aylesworth came daily to hold prayer services. It was little enough to do, but it was all there was left for him.

When the death of Mayor Hilliard became known, Sheriff Johnson called an immediate session of the councilmen and announced himself as Hilliard's successor. Visitors were invited, and Professor Maddox thought it of sufficient importance to attend.

The tension in the air was heavy as the group sat in thick coats in the unheated hall. Johnson spoke without preliminaries. "There are some of you who won't like this," he said. "Our town charter calls for an emergency election in case of the Mayor's death, and some of you think we should have one now.

"So do those out there." He waved a hand toward the window and the town beyond. "However, we're not going to have an election, and I'll tell you why. I know the man who would win it and you do, too. Frank Meggs.

"He hated Hilliard, he hates us, and he hates this town, and he'll do everything in his power to destroy it. Today he would win an election if it were held. He's used the discomfort of the people to stir them to a frenzy against Hilliard's policy of protection for College Hill. He'll stir them up against anything that means a sacrifice of present safety for long-range survival. Meggs is a dangerous man.

"Maybe this isn't the way it ought to be done, but I don't know any other way. When this is all over there will be time enough for elections, and if I don't step down you can shoot me or run me out of the country or anything else you like. For the time being, though, this is the way things are going to be. It's what Hilliard wanted, and I've got his written word if any of you care to see it."

He looked about challengingly. There was a scuffling of feet. Some councilmen looked at their neighbors and back again to the Sheriff. None stood up to speak, nor did any of the visitors voice objections, although several of Frank Meggs' lieutenants were in the group.

"We'll carry on, then," Sheriff Johnson said, "just as before. Food rations will remain as they are. We don't know how many of us there will be after this epidemic is over. Maybe none of us will be here by spring; we can only wait and see."

Although his assumption of power was accepted docilely by the Council, it sparked a furor among the populace of Mayfield. Frank Meggs fanned it with all the strength of his hatred for the town and all it stood for.

Granny Wicks' fortunetelling business continued to grow. Considerations had been given to the desirability of putting a stop to it, but this would have meant literally imprisoning her, and, it was reasoned, this would stir up more fire than it would put out.

Her glory was supreme as she sat in an old rocker in the cottage where she lived. Lines of visitors waited all day at her door. Inside, she was wrapped in a blanket and wore an ancient shawl on her head against the cold of the faintly heated room. She cackled in her high-pitched voice with hysterical glee.

To those who came, her words were solemn pronouncements of eternal truth. To anyone else it would have been sheer mumbo jumbo, but her believers went away in ecstasy after carefully copying her words. They spent hours at home trying to read great meanings into her senile nonsense.

It was quite a time before Frank Meggs realized the power that lay in the old woman, and he berated himself for not recognizing it earlier. When he finally did go to see her, he was not disappointed. It was easy to understand how she, with her ancient, wrinkled face and deep-black eyes, could be confused with a source of prophecy and wisdom in these times of death and terror.

"I want to lead this people, Granny," he said, after she had bade him sit down. "Tell me what to do."

She snorted and eyed him sharply. "What makes you think you can lead this people?" she demanded.

"Because I see they have been led into disaster by selfish, ignorant fools," said Frank Meggs; "men who believe that in the laboratories on the hill there can be found a way to dispel the power of the great comet. Because they believe this, they have persecuted the people. They have taken their food and have given it to the scientists. They have protected them, and them alone, from the disease that sickens us.

"You do not believe these men can overcome the power of the comet, do you, Granny?"

Wild flame leaped in the old woman's eyes. "Nothing can overwhelm the power of this heavenly messenger! Death shall come to all who attempt such blasphemy!"

"Then you will give your blessing to my struggle to release the people from this bondage?"

"Yes!" Granny Wicks spoke with quivering intensity. "You are the man I have been waiting for. I can see it now! You are appointed by the stars themselves!

"I prophesy that you shall succeed and drive out those who dare trifle with the heavens. Go with my blessings, Frank Meggs, and do your great work!"

Elation filled him as he left the house. It was certain that Granny Wicks would pass the word of his "appointment" to all who came to her audience chamber. The way things were going, it looked as if that would be nine-tenths of the people in Mayfield.

The occupation of the Mayor's chair by Sheriff Johnson gave Frank Meggs a further opening that he wanted. The crowds grew at his torchlight harangues. Even though one-third of the population lay ill with the flu, the night meetings went on.

"Sheriff Johnson has no right to the office he holds," he screamed. His appreciative audience huddled in their miserable coldness and howled their agreement.

"This is not the way things should be done. Our charter calls for an election but when will there be an election? My friends, our good Sheriff is not the real villain in this matter. He is but the tool and the dupe of a clever and crafty group who, through him, are the real holders of power and privilege in this town.

"While we have starved, they have been fed in plenty; while we have been cold, they have sat before their warm fires; while we sicken and die of disease, they are immune because the only supply of vaccine in this whole valley was used by them.

"You know who I am talking about! The scientists who would like to rule us, like kings, from the top of College Hill!

"They tell us the comet is responsible for this trouble. But we know different. Who has been responsible for all the trouble the world has known for ages? Science and scientists! The world was once a clean, decent place to live. They have all but destroyed it with their unholy experiments and twistings of nature.

"They've always admitted their atom experiments would make monsters of future generations of men, but they didn't care about that! Now they're frightened because they didn't know these experiments would also destroy the machines on which they had forced us to be dependent. They try to say it is the comet.

"Well, the world would have been better off without their machines in the first place. It would have been better off without them. Now we've got a chance to be free of them at last! Are we going to endure their tyranny from College Hill any longer?"

Night after night, he repeated his words, and the crowds howled their approval.

On College Hill, morale and optimism were at their highest peak since the appearance of the comet. On the roof of Science Hall there was being erected a massive, 30-foot, hyperbolic reflector whose metal surface had been beaten out of aluminum chicken-shed roofs. At its center, and at intervals about the bowl, there projected a series of supersonic generating units, spaced for proper phasing with one another in beaming a concentrated wave of supersonic energy skyward.

Power to this unit was supplied by a motor generator set constructed of decontaminated parts, which had been operating for a full week without sign of breakdown.

Ken and his companions had worked day and night on the rough construction, while the scientists had designed and built the critical supersonic generating equipment. In a solid, 24-hour shift of uninterrupted work they had mounted and tested the units. It was completed on their second day of work. Tomorrow it would be turned on for a full week's run to test the practicability of such a method of precipitating the comet dust.

Laboratory tests had shown it could be done on a small scale. This projector was a pilot model to determine whether it would be worthwhile building a full-size machine with a reflector 250 feet in diameter.

Ken's father looked completely exhausted, but his smile was broader than it had been for many weeks. "I'm confident we will prove the practicability of this machine," he said. "After that, we will build a really big one, and we'll tell the rest of the world how to do it. I don't know how long it will take, but this will do the job. We'll get them to build big ones in Tokyo and Pasadena and Stockholm, wherever there's civilization enough to know how to do it; they can decontaminate their own metals and build new engines that will run as long as necessary. We've got the comet on the run!"

He hadn't meant to give a speech, but he couldn't help it. They were right, and their staggering labors were nearly over, in this phase, at least.

*   *   *   *   *

They slept from exhaustion that night. Ken was awakened in the early-morning hours by the glare in his bedroom window. He sat up and looked out. It seemed to be a very long time before he could let his mind admit what his eyes saw.

Science Hall was in flames, the entire structure a mass of leaping, boiling fire.

Ken ran from his room, crying the alarm.

In their separate rooms, his father and Dr. Larsen stared stupidly at the flickering light as if also unable to comprehend the vastness of the ruin. In frenzy of haste, they donned their clothes and ran from their rooms.

Maria was awake as was Mrs. Maddox. "What is it?" they called. Then they, too, saw the flames through the windows.

The men ran from the house, hatless, their tousled hair flying in the night. Halfway up the hill, Ken called to his father, "You've got to stop, Dad! Don't run like that!"

Professor Maddox came to a halt, his breath bursting from him in great gasps. Ken said, "There's nothing we can do, Dad."

Dr. Larsen stopped beside them. "Nothing except watch," he agreed.

Slowly, they resumed their way. Behind, they heard the sounds of others attracted by the fire. As they came at last to the brow of the hill, Ken pointed in astonishment. "There's a crowd of people over there! Near the burning building!"

He started forward. A shot burst in the night, and a bullet clipped the tree over his head. He dropped to the ground. "Get down! They're firing at us!"

As they lay prone, sickness crept through them simultaneously. "I know who it is," Ken cried. "Frank Meggs. That crazy Frank Meggs! He's got a mob together and fired the college buildings!"

In agony of spirit they crawled to the safety of the slope below the brow of the hill. "We've got to go after Sheriff Johnson," said Ken. "We've got to fight again; we've got to fight all over again!"

Dr. Larsen watched the fire in hypnotic fascination. "All gone," he whispered. "Everything we've done; everything we've built. Our records, our notes. There's nothing left at all."

They moved down the hill, cautioning others about the mob. Sheriff Johnson was already starting up as they reached the bottom. Quickly, they told him what they'd found at the top. "We shouldn't let the mob get off the hill," said Ken. "If we do, we'll never know which ones took part."

"There are as many down here who would like to be up there," said Johnson. "You can be sure of that. We don't know who we can trust any more. Get your science club boys together and find as many patrolmen as possible. Ask each one to get fifteen men he thinks he can trust and meet here an hour from now. If we can do it in that time we may stand a chance of corralling them. Otherwise, we'll never have a chance at them."

"We can try," said Ken.

By now, others had been fired upon and driven back, so that the situation was apparent to everyone. A great many townspeople, most of those well enough to leave their houses, were streaming toward College Hill.

It would be futile to try to find the patrolmen at their own homes, Ken knew. They'd be coming this way, too. He soon found Joe Walton and Al Miner. They mingled in the crowd, calling out for other members of the club. Within minutes, all but two had been found. Word was passed to them to carry out the Sheriff's instructions.

It was easier than they anticipated. Within 20 minutes a dozen officers had been given the word to find their men. At the end of the hour they were gathered and ready for the advance.

The spectators had been driven back. The armed men fanned out to cover the entire hill in a slowly advancing line. They dwindled and became silhouettes against the flames.

At the top, Sheriff Johnson called out to the mob through an improvised megaphone. "Give up your arms and come forward with your hands up!" he cried. "In 10 seconds we start shooting!"

His command was answered by howls of derision. It was like the cries of maniacs, and their drifted words sounded like, "Kill the scientists!"

Bullets accompanied the shouts and howls. The Sheriff's men took cover and began a slow and painful advance.

There could be a thousand mobbers on top of the hill, Ken thought. The Sheriff's men might be outnumbered several times over. He wondered if they ought to try to get reinforcements, and decided against it unless word should be sent down from the top.

There was no way of telling how the battle was going. Gunfire was continuous. A freezing wind had come up and swept over the length of the valley and over those who waited and those who fought. It fanned the flames to volcanic fury.

Ken touched his father's arm. "There's no use for you to stay in this cold," he said. "You ought to go back to the house."

"I've got to know how it comes out up there, who wins."

The cold starlight of the clear sky began to fade. As dawn approached, the flames in the college buildings had burned themselves out. But the gunfire continued almost without letup. Then, almost as quickly as it had started, it died.

After a time, figures appeared on the brow of the hill and came down in a weary procession. Sheriff Johnson led them. He stopped at the bottom of the hill.

"Was it Meggs?" Ken asked. "Did you get Frank Meggs?"

"He fell in the first 10 minutes," said Johnson. "It wasn't really Meggs keeping them going at all. They had a witch up there. As long as she was alive nothing would stop them."

"Granny Wicks! Was she up there?"

"Sitting on a kind of throne they'd made for her out of an old rocking chair. Right in the middle of the whole thing."

"Did she finally get shot?"

Sheriff Johnson shook his head. "She was a witch, a real, live witch. Bullets wouldn't touch her. The west wall of Science Hall collapsed and buried her. That's when they gave up.

"So maybe you can say you won, after all," he said to Professor Maddox. "It's a kind of symbol, anyway, don't you think?"

19
CONQUEST OF THE COMET

For the first time since the coming of the comet, Ken sensed defeat in his father. Professor Maddox seemed to believe at last that they were powerless before the invader out of space. He seemed like a runner who has used his last reserve of strength to reach a goal on which his eye has been fixed, only to discover the true goal is yet an immeasurable distance ahead.

Professor Maddox had believed with all his heart and mind that they had hurdled the last obstacle with the construction of the pilot projector. With it gone, and all their tools and instruments and notes, there was simply nothing.

As Ken considered the problem, it seemed to him the situation was not as bad as first appeared. The most important thing had not been lost. This was the knowledge, locked in their own minds, of what means could prevail against the dust. Beyond this, the truly essential mechanical elements for starting over again were also available.

Art Matthews had been very busy, and he had parts enough for six more motor-generator sets. These were decontaminated and sealed in protective packing. It would be only a matter of hours to assemble one of them, and that would power any supersonic projector they might choose to build.

And they *could* still choose to build one. In the radio supply stores of the town, and in the junk boxes of the members of the science club, there were surely enough components to build several times over the necessary number of generator elements. In the barns and chicken sheds of the valley there was plenty of aluminum sheeting to build reflectors.

The more he considered it, the more possible it seemed to take up from where they had left off the night before the fire. There was one important question Ken asked himself, however: Why stop with a replica of the small pilot model they had built on the roof of Science Hall?

As long as they were committed to building a projector to test for effectiveness, they might as well build a full-scale instrument, one that could take its place as an actual weapon against the dust. If there were errors of design, these could be changed during or after construction. He could see no reason at all for building a mere 30-foot instrument again.

The greatest loss suffered in the fire was that of the chemistry laboratory and its supplies and reagents. Materials for running tests on the dust could not be replaced, nor could much of their microchemical apparatus. The electron microscope, too, was gone. These losses would have to be made up, where necessary, by having such work done by Pasadena, Schenectady or Detroit. If the projector were as successful as all preliminary work indicated, there would be little need for further testing except as a matter of routine check on the concentration of dust in the atmosphere.

Before approaching his father, Ken talked it over with his fellow members of the science club. He wanted to be sure there was no loophole he was overlooking.

"Labor to build the reflector is what we haven't got," said Joe Walton. "It would take months, maybe a whole year, for us to set up only the framework for a 250-foot bowl!"

"Getting the lumber alone would be a community project," said Al.

"That's what it's going to be," Ken answered. "Johnson is behind us. He'll give us anything we want, if he knows where to get it. I don't think there's any question of his authorizing the construction by the men here."

There was nothing else they could think of to stand in the way of the project.

It had been two days since the fire, but Ken's father still seemed stunned by it. After dinner, he sat in his old chair where he used to read, but he did not read now. He sat for hours, staring at the opposite corner of the room.

Professor Larsen seemed locked in a similar state of shock. In addition to his wife's death, this destruction of their entire scientific facilities seemed a final blow from which he could not recover.

Ken recognized, too, that there was a burden these men had carried that no one else knew. That was the burden of top-level responsibility for a major portion of the world's effort against the "invader." It was an Atlas-like burden that men could not carry without suffering its effects.

Ken approached them that evening, after he and Maria had helped his mother with her chores and had gathered snow to melt overnight for their next day's water supply.

"Dad," Ken said, "I've been wondering when we could get started on the project again. The fellows in the club are all ready to go. I guess most everyone else is, too."

His father looked as if Ken had just uttered something absolutely unintelligible. "Start!" he cried. "Start what? How can we start anything? There's nothing left to work with, absolutely nothing!"

Ken hesitated, an ache in his heart at the defeat he saw in his father's eyes. He held out his hands. "We've got these," he said. He tapped the side of his head. "And this."

Professor Maddox's face seemed to relax a trifle. He looked at his son with a faint suggestion of a smile on his lips. "Yes? What do you propose to do with them?"

Carefully, then, Ken outlined the results of his inventory. "Art can build up to six engines, if we need them. We've got plenty of electronic parts, and tubes big enough to put 60 or 70 kilowatts of supersonic energy in a beam. We don't want to build a little reflector again; we want to put up a full-scale instrument. When that's done, build another one, and still another, until we've used every scrap of material available in the valley. By that time maybe we'll have some cars running and can go to Frederick and other towns for more parts."

Ken's father leaned back in his chair, his eyes closed. "If enthusiasm could do it, we could look forward to such a structure the day after tomorrow."

"Maybe enthusiasm *can* do it," said Professor Larsen quietly. "I believe the boy is right. We've let ourselves despair too much because of the fire. We still have the necessary principles in our heads. If Ken is right, we've got the materials. The only problem is that you and I are a pair of old, exhausted men, without the necessary enthusiasm and energy. Perhaps we can borrow enough of that from these boys. I'm in favor of undertaking it!"

By the light of oil lamps they planned and talked until far past midnight. There were still no objections to be found outside the labor problem. When they were through, rough drawings and calculations for the first projector were finished.

"Such a projector could surely reach well into the stratosphere," said Professor Larsen. "With the tremendous velocities of the air masses at those heights, one projector should be able to process hundreds of tons of atmosphere per day."

"I am wondering," said Professor Maddox, "if we should not make the reflector parabolic instead of hyperbolic. We may disperse our energy too widely to be effective at high levels."

"I think not. The parabola would narrow the beam to little more than its initial diameter and would concentrate the energy more than is required. With the power Ken speaks of, I believe the hyperbolic form could carry an effective wave into the stratosphere. We'll make some calculations for comparison tomorrow."

*   *   *   *   *

They authorized Ken to speak with the Sheriff the following day.

"I've been wondering when I'd see some of you people," Johnson said bluntly. "What are you doing about the mess on the hill?"

"My father thought maybe you'd drop in," said Ken.

The Sheriff shook his head. "It's your move. I just wondered if you had any ideas, or if this fire had knocked the props out from under you."

"It did, but now we're ready to go, and we need help." Briefly, Ken gave a description of the projector they planned to build. "Labor is the problem for us. If we could have all the carpenters in town, and all who could be spared from woodcutting and every other activity for 2 or 3 weeks I think we could get it done."

"You know how many men are left," said Johnson. "Between the war with the nomads and the epidemic of flu, one-third of those we had when this started are dead. A third of the ones left are sick, and quite a few of those on their feet have to take care of the ones that aren't."

"I know," said Ken.

"You know how the people feel about you scientists?"

"Yes."

The Sheriff stared at him a long time before continuing. "It won't be easy, but we'll do it. When do you want to start?"

"Tomorrow morning. In Jenkin's pasture, north of town."

"How many men?"

"All the carpenters you can get and a hundred others to rustle materials and tear down old buildings."

"I meet with the Council this afternoon to go over work assignments. You'll have your men in the morning."

The rest of the day, Ken and his fellow club members chose the exact spot to erect the projector and staked it out. They spotted the nearest buildings that could be dismantled for materials, and made estimates of how much they needed.

The following morning they met again on the site, and there were ten men from town, in addition to the college students and others who had taken part in the research on College Hill.

"Are you all Johnson could spare?" Ken asked the group.

The nearest man shook his head. "They were assigned. No one else would come. They think you are wasting your time; they think you can't do anything about the comet. A lot of them are like Meggs and Granny Wicks: they think you shouldn't *try* to do anything about it."

Ken felt a blaze of anger. "Sometimes, I think they're right!" he said bitterly. "Maybe it would be better if we just let the whole thing go!"

"Now don't get me wrong," the man said. "We're on your side. We're here, aren't we? I'm just telling you what they say and think in town."

"I know and I'm sorry. These other fellows will tell you what we need done. I'm going to ride in to see Johnson."

The Sheriff was not in his office. Ken was told he had gone over to the food warehouse where rations were being distributed. There was some rumor of a disturbance.

Ken remounted his horse and rode to the warehouse. As he approached, he saw the lineup before the distribution counter was motionless. In front of the counter, Sheriff Johnson stood with a pair of revolvers in his hands, holding back the crowd.

He glanced at Ken and said, "Don't tell me! I know you haven't any workers out there today. They're here in line, trying to collect groceries without working!"

"We're not going to work so those scientists on the hill can have the fat of everything!" a man near the head of the line shouted. Others echoed him with cries of hysteria.

Ken felt his disgust and disappointment vanish before a wave of genuine fear. These people had ceased to be anything but frightened, hungry animals. Their capacity for rational action had all but disappeared under the strains they had suffered. They were ready to lash out at anything that appeared a suitable target for their own hysterical anger and panic.

It was useless to expect them to help with the projector. The crew of scientists and students would have to do it alone, no matter how many weeks it took.

Sheriff Johnson, however, had no such thought. He fired a bullet over the heads of the crowd and brought them to silence. "Listen to me," he said. "I know you're sick and hungry and scared. There's not a man or woman in this valley who isn't, and that includes me and the members of the Council, and those you tried to burn off College Hill.

"You don't know how good you've got it! You don't deserve it as good as you've got. You people should have been with those in Chicago or in San Francisco. You should have known what it was really like to be suddenly cut off from every ounce of food beyond that which was in your own cupboards. You should have known what it was like to fight day after day in the streets of a burning city without knowing why you were fighting, or having any hope of victory.

"You've gone through your battle, and you've won, and you're still here, and there's food left. A lot of us are still going to die before the epidemic is over. We haven't the medical means to save us all. But some of us will come out of it, and every one has just as good a chance as his neighbor.

"That's not important. It doesn't make much difference whether any one of us stays alive now, or dies in 50 years. What is important is trying to keep the world alive, and that's what these scientists are doing.

"While you accuse them of every crime in the book, they are the only chance the world has got for survival!"

"They can't do anything about it!" a woman shouted. "They're just making it up to get more than the rest of us!"

The crowd started to take up its cry again.

"Shut up!" the Sheriff thundered at them. "I repeat: you don't deserve to be as lucky as you are! But you aren't going to get out of taking your part in pulling things back together again. Help is needed out there north of town, and you're going to help.

"You help or you don't eat!"

A roar of rage thundered from the group. One man stepped forward. "You can't pull a thing like this, Johnson. We've got guns, too. We've used them before, and we can use them again!"

"Then you had better go home and get them right now," said Johnson. "My men and I will be waiting for you. I suppose there could be a lot more of you than there are of us, so you can probably shoot us down. Then you can eat all you want for a month, and die. Go get your gun, Hank, and come after your rations!"

The man turned to the crowd. "Okay, you heard what he said! Let's go and get 'em!"

He strode away, then turned back to beckon his followers. In the empty street before the converted theater, he stood alone. "Come on!" he cried. "Who's coming with me?"

The crowd avoided his eyes. They shifted uneasily and looked at Johnson again. "What do you mean?" another man asked. "About, we work or we don't eat—"

"Come on, you guys!" Hank shouted.

"The assignments on the projector will be rotated," said Johnson. "We'll spare as many men as we can from everything else. Those of you who have been given assignment slips will get 3 days' rations. When you bring back the slips with a verification that you did your job on the projector you'll get an assignment somewhere else until it's your turn again. The ones without verification on the slips don't get the next 3 days' rations. That's the way it's going to be. If there's no more argument, we'll get on with the distribution.

"Hank, get down at the end of the line!"

By mid-afternoon, the scientists had their full crew of sullen and unwilling helpers. The Sheriff had sent along a half-dozen of his own men, fully armed, to see there was no disturbance, but the objectors seemed to have had their say.

With a gradual increase of co-operativeness, they did the tasks they were assigned, bringing up materials, laying out the first members of the great, skeletal structure that would rise in the pasture. Johnson came at the end of the day to see how it was going. He breathed a sigh of relief at the lack of disturbance. "It looks like we've got it made," he said.

"I think so," Ken agreed. "All we have to do now is see how many more of these we can get built in other parts of the world."

They spoke that night to all the stations on the radio net, describing in detail what they had begun, what they were confident it would do. Professor Larsen's words were relayed to his colleagues in Stockholm. They estimated they could begin work almost immediately on six projectors. Others, elsewhere in the country, were quite probable.

In his conversation with Pasadena, Professor Maddox warned, "We have not yet been able to make tests with the big projector. Our only work so far has been with the laboratory models, but they were highly successful."

"That's good enough for us," said Dr. Whitehead, director of the Pasadena work. "Everything we've done here has failed so far. A direct chemical approach seems out of the question. We'll start with one, but I think a dozen projectors, at least, are possible for this area."

Pasadena also reported a new radio contact with Calcutta, and promised to pass the word on to them and to Tokyo. When they closed down the transmitter after midnight, Ken totaled the number of projectors promised with reasonable certainty of having the promises fulfilled. There were eighty.

"It may take a year," his father said, "or it may take 10 years, but now we know, without a doubt, that we can someday get our atmosphere back as it was before the comet."

20
RECONSTRUCTION

On the twentieth of January the comet reached its closest approach to Earth. It was then less than three million miles away. In the realm of the stars, this was virtually a collision, and if the head of the comet had been composed of anything more than highly rarefied gases it would have caused tremendous upheavals and tidal waves.

There were none of these. Only the dust.

Ken arose at dawn that day and went into the yard to watch the rising of the golden enemy a little before the sun came over the eastern hills. He doubted whether anyone else was aware it was closer today than it had been before, or ever would be again. He doubted there would be much scientific interest in the event, anywhere in the world.

In the observatory, he opened the dome and adjusted the telescope to take a few pictures and spectrograms. He remembered when he had done this, a long time ago, with high excitement and curiosity, and he remembered later times when he had looked up with a bitter hate in his heart for the impersonal object in the sky.

Now, he felt nothing. He was aware only of a kind of deadness in his emotions with respect to the comet.

There was no excitement he could find in today's event of close approach, which was probably the only one of its kind that would be recorded in the history of mankind. He wondered if he had lost all his scientific spirit that so momentous an occurrence could inspire him so little now.

Yet, he no longer hated the comet, either. It was not a thing that could be hated, any more than the wind when it leveled a city, or the waters when they drowned the land and the people on it.

These things were beyond hate. You could fight them, but you never had the privilege of hating them. That was reserved only for other human beings. It was because of the great, impersonal nature of their common enemy, he thought, that people had finally turned to fighting each other. It was for this reason that the people of Mayfield had turned their hate upon the scientists. The questions of food and privileges were only superficial excuses.

After an hour's work, Ken left the observatory. The gassy tail of the comet was a full halo of lighter yellow hue, as seen directly along its central axis. The darker yellow of the core seemed to Ken like a living heart.

The light spread to the dust motes in the air and curtained the whole sky with shimmering haze. It bathed the snow cover of the Earth, and reflected its golden image against the trees and the walls of the buildings, and penetrated the windows. It gilded the stark, charcoal skeletons of the ruins it had created. It spread over the whole Earth and penetrated every pore. Ken had a momentary illusion that there was not a particle of substance in the world not permeated and illumined by the comet's light. He felt as if it were inside his own being, through his vitals, and shining in the corridors of his brain.

For a moment the old hate returned. He wanted to shut his eyes against that omnipresent light and to run with all his strength to some secret place where it could never penetrate.

He recalled the words of Dr. Larsen that seemed to have been uttered so long ago that they were scarcely within memory: "The universe is a terrible place that barely tolerates living organisms. It is a great miracle that here in this corner of the universe living things have found a foothold. It does not pay ever to forget the fierceness of the home in which we live."

There was no closing the eyes against this. He looked again at the comet, the representative to Earthmen of all the fierceness and terror that lay in outer space, beyond the thin tissue of atmosphere that protected man and his fragile life. He would remember all the days of his life that the universe might be beautiful and exciting and terrible, but whatever it was, it held no friendliness toward man. It could destroy him with a mere whim of chance occurrence. Man had gained a foothold, but there was a long way to go to an enduring security.

*   *   *   *   *

On the day of the official beginning of operation of the giant projector in Jenkin's pasture, there was a little ceremony. Sheriff Johnson stood on an improvised platform and with an impressive gesture threw the switch that officially turned the power into the great instrument. It had been successfully tested previously, but now it was launched in an operation that would not cease until the last trace of comet dust had fallen from the sky and was mingled with the dust of the Earth.

Most of the townspeople who were well enough to do so turned out for the ceremony. During the construction, a guard had been kept to prevent sabotage of the projector, but there had been no attempts made on it. Now the people stood in the trampled snow and ice of the pasture, staring up at the giant structure, with a quality of near-friendliness in their eyes and in the expressions of their faces.

The Sheriff made a little speech after throwing the switch. He thanked them for their co-operation and thousands of man-hours of labor, not mentioning that it had been obtained, initially, at the point of his guns. He praised the scientists and noted that conquest of the comet might never have been achieved without the genius of their men of College Hill. He did not mention the attempts to destroy that genius.

"I think we should all like to hear," he said, "from the man who has led this vast and noble effort from its inception. He will speak for all those who have worked so steadfastly to bring this effort to a successful conclusion. Professor Maddox!"

There was a flurry of applause. Then it grew, and a shout went up. They called his name and cheered as he stood, a figure dwarfed against the background of the great projector bowl.

Ken knew what he must be thinking as he waited for the cheers to subside. He must be thinking: they have forgotten already, forgotten the angers and the jealousies and the fears, their attempts to destroy the small kernel of scientific hope in their midst. They had forgotten everything but the warming belief that perhaps the worst of the terror was over and they had lived through it.

"I'm grateful," Professor Maddox was saying, "for the assistance you have given this project, although you had no personal knowledge of what it was meant to do. We asked for your faith and we asked for your confidence that we knew what we were about, at a time when we did not know it even for ourselves. We were nourished and cared for at your expense in order that our work might go on. It would not have succeeded without you."

Ken realized his father was not speaking ironically but meant just what he said. And it was true.

The vengeful Meggs and the psychotic Granny Wicks had fought them and incited others who were frightened beyond reason. Yet there had been Hilliard and Johnson, the Council, and many others who had supported them. There were those who had built the projector, even though at the point of a gun, and at the threat of starvation. All of them together had made the project possible.

It was a miniature of the rise of the whole human race, Ken supposed. More like a single individual with a multitude of psychoses, hopes, and geniuses, than a group of separate entities, they had come to this point. In the same way, they would go on, trying to destroy the weaknesses and multiply their strength.

* * * * *

By the middle of February the flu epidemic was over. Its toll had leveled the population to a reasonable balance with the food supply. Whether Mayor Hilliard's ironic suggestion reflected any real principle or not, the situation had worked out in accord with his macabre prediction.

Ken had explained the comet's daily infinitesimal retreat and there was a kind of steady excitement in estimating how much it diminished each day. Actually, a week's decrease was too small for the naked eye to detect, but this did not matter.

Radio reports continued to tell of increased construction of projectors throughout the world. Tests were showing they were effective beyond all previous hopes.

The populace of Mayfield was enthusiastic about the construction of additional units. Two more had been built, and three others were planned. Serious attention had to be given now to the coming planting season. Every square foot of available ground would have to be cultivated to try to build up stores for all possible emergencies of the following winter.

When the time came for making the first work assignments on the farms, Professor Maddox and Professor Larsen appeared to receive theirs. Sheriff Johnson was in the office at the time. "What are you two doing here? You can get back to your regular business," he stormed. "We aren't that hard up for farmers!"

"We have no regular business," said Professor Maddox. "The projector work is being taken care of. Mayfield will probably not be the site of a university again during our lifetimes. We want to be assigned some acres to plow. By the way, did you hear Art Matthews has got three more tractors in operation this week? If we can find enough gasoline we may be able to do the whole season's plowing by machine."

"You're sure you want to do this?" said Sheriff Johnson.

"Quite sure. Just put our names down as plain dirt farmers."

*   *   *   *   *

Ken clung to the radio for reports of the outside world. The batteries were all but exhausted, but a motor generator could be allotted to the station as soon as other work was out of the way.

In Pasadena, they told him a diesel railway engine had been successfully decontaminated and put into operation. Airtight packing boxes had been designed for the wheels to keep them from being freshly affected by the dust remaining in the air. It was planned to operate a train from the metropolitan area to the great farming sections to the east and north. A few essential manufactures had also been revived, mostly in the form of machine shops to decontaminate engine parts.

Negotiations were under way to try to move the great wheat and other grain stocks of the Midwest down the Mississippi River to New Orleans and through the Panama Canal to the Pacific Coast cities. Oldtime sailing vessels, rotting from years of disuse, were being rebuilt for this purpose.

Ken found it hard to envision the Earth stirring with this much life after the destruction that had passed over it. In the civilized areas, it was estimated that fully two-thirds of the population had perished. Only in the most primitive areas had the comet's effect been lightly felt. Yet, around the world, the cities were stirring again. Food for the surviving was being found. The hates and the terrors were being put away and men were pulling together again to restore their civilization.

Maria came to the radio shack to tell him dinner was ready. He invited her to join him for a moment. "It may be possible for you and your father to return to Sweden much sooner that we thought," he said.

Maria shook her head. "We aren't going back, now. We've talked about it and decided to stay. It's as Papa always said: Where so much happens to you, that's the place you always call home. More has happened to us in a year here than in a lifetime back there."

Ken laughed. "That's a funny way to look at it, especially after the kind of things that have happened to you here. Maybe your father is right, at that."

"All our friends are here now," she said.

"All I can say is that it's wonderful," Ken said with a rising surge of happiness in him. "I mean," he added in sudden confusion, "I'm glad you've decided this is the best place to live."

He changed the subject quickly. "Dad's even talking of trying to start up a kind of college here again. We wouldn't have the buildings, of course, but it could be done in houses or somewhere else. He says he's been thinking a lot about it and considers it would be our greatest mistake to neglect the continuance of our education. So I guess you can finish school right here.

"Personally, I think all the professors out there trying to be dirt farmers just got tired after a couple of days of plowing and decided something would have to be done about *that* situation!"

Maria laughed. "Don't be too hard on them. Papa told me about the plan, too. He says Sheriff Johnson has agreed to guarantee their pay in food and other necessities. He's stepping down now, so there can be an election, but he's demanding approval of that program before he leaves office. I don't think they ought to let him go."

"He'll be re-elected," said Ken. "He's on top of the heap now. I even heard old Hank Moss chewing out some guys in town for criticizing Johnson!"

Ken closed down the transmitter and receiver for the night. Together, he and Maria walked to the house. They stopped on the back porch and glanced toward the distant projector bowls reflecting the light of the comet and of the sun.

Soon there would be only the sun to shine in the sky. The Earth was alive. Man was on his way up again.

THE END

And Now a Message . . .
By Greg Fowlkes

A short Story from the upcoming Book - *Back Road to the Stars*

And Now A Message . . .

For the third time that night Jack Olsen was about to
nod off over the copy of *Statistical Information Theory*
that he was attempting to read. Giving it up as a bad
effort, he shut the book and looked out the window of the
control room at the giant bowl of the Arecibo radio
telescope. Theoretically he was running the huge
instrument, but in reality all the controlling was being
done by the computers in the room around him. For six
months he had been working eight hour shifts every
night, and his job had consisted of the five minutes a shift
that it took to enter the coordinates to be examined on
the control console. Other than that, he was on hand only
for the off chance that the monitoring programs would
recognize some pattern in the radio noise, in which case
an alarm would sound. So far, in the six months, it
hadn't happened.

He walked over to the coffee machine in the hopes
that a cup would revive him enough so that he could
continue his studies. He never made it, for as if to prove
the lie of his earlier thoughts, the alarm sounded. For a
moment Jack was frozen, the alarm beating raucously in
his ears, then he pulled himself together and flicked off
the switch on the bell. With the room returned to the
relative quiet of the whoosh of the cooling fans on the
equipment, Jack sat down at the console and keyed in an
enquiry. Within seconds the computer had replied that it
was receiving a strong periodic signal on the 42
centimeter band. Further questioning showed that it was
not a program malfunction but a genuine signal.

Jack picked up the phone and dialed his boss's number. It was three in the morning, but his instructions had been clear. If anything was received that could possibly be an intelligent signal, he was supposed to contact his superior immediately.

Despite the long drive through the mountains in the cool Puerto Rican night, Professor Kraft showed up with his eyes still sleepy. Shuffling over to the coffee pot by the window he poured himself a large mug before he said anything. "You'd better have something good to get me up at this hour."

"I think so," Jack said, aware that his boss's irritation was only feigned. "I've been checking with the computer since I called you. It shows a strong periodic signal with a sharp pulse every fifty milliseconds. It runs on like that for about two and a half minutes before the signal fades below the background."

"Any chance that it might be a pulsar?" Kraft asked, referring to the radio signals of rapidly rotating neutron stars. "That's within the range of periods for them. When the first one was discovered, they thought that they had received intelligent signals."

"I thought of that, so I checked the record of the broad band receiver." Jack brought out a long strip of graph paper and pointed to the evenly spaced patterns of peaks on it. "Where the narrow band shows only a single repetitive pulse, the wide band gives us this fine structure. It's far too regular to be a pulsar and much too detailed. It's more like some sort of timing signal or spacer. And in between the pulses there is another signal. It's not as repetitive as the main pulse. That's why the program doesn't bring it out. But there definitely is some sort of transmission in between. It's weaker, but I think that we can write a processing program to pick it out from the noise."

Kraft looked at the trace in his hand thoughtfully. "I hate to make snap judgements. You can be suckered in too easily that way. But it does look like some kind of artificial signal. We'll get the team working on it in the morning. Have you received any additional signals?"

"No. I've kept the dish tracking the source, but all we get on 42 cm. is background noise. It's like there was a moment of freak atmospheric conditions that opened a window, and then it shut again. Just like you get with shortwave sometimes because of the ionosphere."

"Well, we should be grateful for what we've got. I don't think I can sleep anymore tonight, so I'll keep you company. I'd like to be here if we get any more messages from our friends out there," he said, pointing with his cup towards the star filled sky that loomed over the radio telescope's antenna.

"Frustrating, isn't it?" Prof. Kraft remarked to the team of graduate students and post doctoral fellows that were working under him on the interstellar communications project. And frustrating it had been. For six months they had continuously monitored the sky searching for signs of life finally to be rewarded by a two minute snippet of extraterrestrial conversation.

Now, another six months later, they had still made no sense of the signal, nor had they received any further transmissions from that part of the sky, though they had concentrated their efforts in that direction.

"Rumors have leaked out about our discovery, and I've been getting requests for the data. I'd sure hate to have someone else steal our thunder by deciphering the signal, but if we don't make some progress soon, we're going to have to release it." He looked around the table at the young faces of his assistants. At the moment they didn't look nearly as bright and intelligent as he knew they were.

"Why don't I summarize what we've found so far in hopes that it will give us some new ideas?"

"First, we've got this repetitive pattern of pulses every twentieth of a second as regular as clockwork. So regular, in fact, that we can't decide whether they serve as breaks in the message or were just put there to attract our attention. Remember, it was these pulses that were first recognized by the computer."

"But the pulses aren't the real message. That lays in the spaces in between. We've been able to deduce that the messages are digitized and the computer has been able to enhance them so that we have a fairly error free record of them. There is some repetitive structure to them, and they do vary in some sort of progression, but beyond that, we haven't been able to get the least notion of what they mean. Anyone have something to add?"

Bill Warden, one of the post docs, spoke up. "Well, we've tried mathematical analysis on the signals and have gotten zero results. It has already been assumed that any sort of interstellar communications would be based on sort of easily recognizable mathematical progression. Like one, two three. Something like that to show that they were rational. From there you can always build up more complicated concepts."

"With this message we don't have that, which leads us to one of two assumptions. One, we have only a fragment of a broadcast, and from a very advanced lesson at that. If that's the case, I don't see much hope of our being able to decipher the message until we can receive more signals to give us a broader base to work from."

"The other alternative is that they, whoever they are, just don't think like us. Their minds work in some fashion so that this mess we have makes sense to them. If so, I don't see any hope at all. Their minds may just be too foreign for us to hold a dialog with them."

"Thank you for that optimistic note," Prof. Kraft said wryly. "For the first time mankind has received a message from another species and we can't tell whether it is a cure for cancer, a means of achieving universal peace, or a recipe for sauerbratten. Any comments?"

"If it's sauerbratten, where do we go for a tablespoon of powdered bandersnatch egg?" quipped one of the grad students. They all laughed at the joke more than it deserved. Six months of unrewarded work had left them all a little giddy. After the giggles and comments had died down, Jack Olsen coughed, trying to get their attention.

"You've got something useful to say, Jack?" Kraft asked. "You might as well tell us. I don't think anyone else has anything useful to add," he said, pointedly looking at the wisecracker.

"I've been thinking about the signal, and I remember something that I said to you the night it came in. I don't know if you recall, but I called the pulses timing signals. Now there is one type of common transmission that has the same kind of pulses, and that's television. They use the pulses to synchronize the frames. It's possible that the message in between each pulse is a picture, and the whole transmission is meant to be viewed in sequence."

"How long have you been sitting on this while the rest of us were beating our brains out?" Kraft asked.

"It just came to me," Jack said, his face flushed. "I should have thought of it earlier, but like Bill said, we've all been conditioned to look for something like one plus one equals two."

"I think that we should all have seen it," Kraft said. "It makes as much sense as anything else that's been suggested. Do you think that you can get us a picture?"

"If it's there, I should be able to pick it out using the computer," Jack answered.

"Good. Then, since it was your idea, you're in charge. Dragoon anything or anybody that you need to help you."

Five days later they were all gathered around the conference room table again, but this time there was a TV set and a video recorder on a cart at its end. From the nervous stubbing of cigarette butts and fingers drumming on the table, it was obvious that all the members of the team were in a state of anticipation.

"It took some time to figure out exactly how the signal was put together," Jack began. "After all, we didn't know how many lines there were in each frame or how many bits made up each unit of picture. In the end, I had to have the computer run through all the likely possibilities for one of the frames. It took a lot of computer time, but I've finally got some recognizable pictures."

"It turns out that the original broadcast was in color. That threw us for a while, but we finally psyched it out. The aliens must have eyes structurally different from ours; there are only two colors, not three in the signal. Which colors they are is anybody's guess. They might be ultraviolet and infrared for all we can tell. Arbitrarily, I've assigned them red and bluish green, so keep that in mind. Also, because the video recorder uses thirty frames a second instead of the twenty in the transmission, it was necessary to compress the program a bit. This means that everything you'll be seeing has been speeded up about fifty percent.

"I guess you're all more interested in seeing the tape than in listening to me." A snort from Prof. Kraft indicated agreement. Jack flicked off the lights and started the tape. For a minute the screen showed only snow, then a face became recognizable. It was a sickly chartreuse, and there was no nose between the two large, oval eyes, but it was recognizable as a face. The figures movements were quick and jerky like an old silent movie, the result of the difference in frame speed, and the picture left a lot to be desired in clarity, the product of interstellar noise, but it was a picture, the first of an alien race.

As the tape played, a weird, sings song voice came from the speaker sounding something like a Chinese chipmunk. "I forgot to mention that there was also an audio track along with the signal. Again, it's only a reconstruction and may not bear much resemblance to the original, but then, we'll never know," Jack commented. They had determined that the source of the transmission was at least several dozen light years away. It would take twice that number of years to send a message and receive a reply, by which time they would all be dead.

They continued to watch the tape. The camera had drawn back to show the alien from the waist up revealing rounded shoulders and a pair of six fingered hands. Apparently he was standing behind a low lectern or a table of some sort. The fuzzy picture and camera angle made it hard to tell which. As he, or her, or it, spoke, the alien pointed at a chart or poster suspended on the backdrop. A pattern of red and blue that hurt the eye with violent contrasts seemed to be some sort of text. The voice continued as the picture disappeared in a sea of snow and then it broke into static. The transmission had ended.

"You've done a fine job, Jack," Prof. Kraft said after they had played the tape through a half dozen times. "It's actually far better than I thought it would be, and I think we can accept any of the shortcomings that you mentioned."

"So, we've got a face and body of what certainly is a rational creature. He seemed to be giving us a lesson or lecture of some sort, though I for one don't have the faintest idea of what he was talking about. We have an idea of what they look like which I am sure will give the biologists a lot to speculate on, so I guess that we should be thankful for small favors, but I still don't see how we're going to learn any more about them without receiving further signals."

"I wouldn't hold out much hope of that," Jack interjected. "I think that it's clear now that the signal we picked up was not meant for interstellar communication. Any such signal would have been designed with much greater noise immunity. We were able to receive it only because of an accident of atmospheric conditions. It was actually just a local TV broadcast. As we haven't received anything since, those conditions must be rare."

"So," Kraft said, "we have a message of great potential import, that at the very least could provide us with insights on a totally alien culture, and no way to decipher it."

"I've got an idea," Bill said. "We've all been looking at the problem from the point of view of hardware and computer programs. That's natural because of our backgrounds, but now that we have what amounts to an artifact, maybe we should call in a specialist. We need someone who is trained in resurrecting a culture from its fragments. I suggest that we show the tape to some archeologists and get their opinions."

Convincing an archeologist to look at the tape was harder than it had sounded. Most of them were more interested in ancient rather than alien civilizations. Jack suspected that they felt out of their depth with the computers and electronics. With some pressure and pleading, a group finally agreed to view the tape, but after the showing, only one evinced any interest in following up on it.

A visiting lecturer from Norway, she was reputed to have a good background in languages, though Jack lacked the knowledge to judge her qualifications. However, as she was young, blond, and attractive, he was quite willing to spend the time required to familiarize her with the tape and the equipment they had used to come up with it. Together, they spent hours viewing the tape, studying it frame by frame attempting to pick out the slightest piece of information.

The project team had been assembled in the conference room, and this time it was the archeologist's turn to address them. For three weeks Cristina Peterson had been studying the tape almost constantly, and now she was ready to give her opinion. With the exception of Jack, who had been working closely with her, they were all, even Prof. Kraft, eagerly awaiting the report. There had been a great deal of speculation about what her findings would be.

"First," she began, "before I get your hopes up, I want to say that I have not been able to get a word for word translation of the voice on the tape. The sample of speech is just too brief for that to be possible. If the scene had contained more action, I might have been more successful, but we were not that fortunate. I have, however, been able to form a hypothesis based on the spoken word as well as visual clues such as facial expression, setting, and so on."

"An important point to remember is that the aliens, despite certain differences in appearance, are not too dissimilar from ourselves. They are bipedal, intelligent, and possess opposable thumbs. They have binocular vision and a form of color perception as well. Brain size is about the same in relationship to total body size as in humans, and I would be greatly surprised if they were much larger or smaller than ourselves. That much can be guessed on the basis of physiology from the picture and the nature of the signal. From this information, I think that we can draw the conclusion that their planet is, within limits, earthlike."

"Probably more relevant is their state of culture. They obviously have a technology and one that is recognizable in terms of our own. That we can receive their signals is proof of that. Also, they speak, they wear clothing, we can even guess at the purpose of some of the objects visible in the tape. I might add that this is more than we can do for some of the artifacts of primitive human cultures. In some ways we have more in common with the aliens than we do with the Tasadi or Bushman."

"I want you to bear in mind that these beings are not greatly different from ourselves. If we are to properly analyze the contents of the message, we must remember that they are influenced by the same drives and forces as humans." There was an uneasy shifting in their seats on the part of the team members as they took in the meaning of her statement.

"If we accept this premise, and replace the alien with a human, we can make an educated guess as to what we are seen on the tape. I'll run it again for you so that you can make the substitution." Jack tapped the switch, and for the next minute and a half they watched the now familiar scene replay itself.

"Before I give my own opinion, would anyone else like to make a guess?" Cristina asked.

Kraft looked around the room, but it appeared as though no one had the courage to be the first to put his own views forward. To break the silence he said, "It's only a guess, but to start the discussion, I'd say that the alien might be a lecturer. He's obviously standing at some sort of podium or speaker's table."

"He seems a little too impassioned for a lecturer, at least in the physical sciences," one of the grad students remarked. "I've never seen you that excited before a class." Kraft smiled at the reference to his own low keyed classroom delivery.

"Maybe it's a political science class. They get more aroused."

Bill Warden broke in, "Why a class? It looks to me more like he's a politician trying to persuade the voters. He must be up for reelection. The sign in back could be an election poster." That brought a couple of laughs and a few less than serious comments.

"We've all had a crack at it," Prof. Kraft said. "You obviously have your own interpretation, and I think that we've been kept in suspense long enough. From the look on Jack's face, it must be a good one. Let's hear it now. After all, the communication between two species is one of the most important events in human history."

She smiled at the jibe. "All your suggestions are plausible, but I've spent more time analyzing the tape than you have. I'll play it again for you and point out the features that have led me to my interpretation."

"The first thing that caught my attention was the fact that the word 'gratach' was mentioned fourteen times, an unusually high incidence in such a brief speech. Furthermore, at least four of those times the speaker pointed to the symbols on the chart behind him. I think that we can assume that 'gratach' is a name, and the symbols form the written version."

"Now here's something that I want you to see." She froze the picture on the television. "Note the artifacts on the table, a bowl filled with a substance and a box or container. There appears to be some writing on the box, but the resolution of the picture isn't good enough to allow us to make it out. However," she said as the tape began to roll again, "as the alien points to the box and says 'gratach' it is likely that the symbols again spell out the name in the chart behind the alien. Note, too, the expression on his face. Despite the lack of a nose, the face is surprisingly human, and if that expression was on a human face, it would be one of approval or pleasure."

"I think that if you put all the clues together, you can come to only one conclusion. Dr. Warden was not far off when he suggested a political campaign. The speaker is definitely trying to persuade his audience, but it is the package, not himself, that he is trying to sell."

"Oh, god," Kraft sputtered. "You can't mean it. The first communication from another planet and it's only . . ."

"Yes, I'm afraid so," Cristina said. "The first and only signal received from another world is nothing more than a breakfast food commercial."

Special Preview!

THE LAWS OF MAGIC
BY GREG FOWLKES
© 2010

Now available from The Fictional Press
www.TheFictionalPress.com

THE LAWS OF MAGIC
WITHOUT LICENSE

☆ ☆ ☆ ☆ ☆

As Egil Njalsson climbed the steps of the criminal courts building he wondered if it was really worth it. Eighteen months of practicing law on his own and here he was in his only suit, about to attend the preliminary hearing in a petty case for which with luck he would be able to recover his expenses. It wasn't even a paying client. The state would be picking up the tab for this one, and he'd ended up being the lawyer appointed by the court. At the moment it wasn't clear who would benefit most from the charity, the client or the lawyer. He hadn't had a case in three months and he'd just been eking out a living writing briefs for other lawyers. He could do that well enough. His technical background gave him a depth of knowledge most lawyers lacked when it came to cases involving points of science as well as law. If he hadn't had that he'd be starving.

He'd been thinking about that a lot lately; whether he had made the right decision giving up science and going into the law. At the time, with the aerospace industry in a depression in the early seventies, it had seemed like a good idea. Engineers were pumping gas and PhD's in physics were selling insurance. Being a lawyer had seemed like a good way to make money. A stable income, no ups and downs. He'd put in his time at law school and done well. After the grind at CalThaum, law school had been a snap. So here he was a lawyer barely making ends meet and his school mates, the ones who had stuck with science were all making it rich designing personal calculating engines and disk storage units.

He tried to put all these thoughts out of his mind as he passed through the big brass doors of the court house. After all, he did have a client to defend, and a duty to him. It wasn't easy, though. It wasn't, after all, a very important case. Just a charge of fortune telling and practicing the Art without a license. Minor offenses, probably not even any jail time involved. This wouldn't even be a trial today, just a plea and arranging of bail.

It wouldn't even have amounted to that if his client hadn't instisted on pleading not guilty. He'd met him at the county jail, an old man, one Jake Schmidts. He'd tried to talk him out of pleading not guilty, too. A guilty plea, a small fine, and they both could be done with it. His client, though, had turned out to be something of a character. So here he was.

It took an hour and a half before their case came up. The judge looked at him questioningly when he had pleaded not guilty, but thankfully had released his client on his own recognizance when he indicated he had a permanent address. It was over in five minutes.

They got the release papers and the court date from the bailiff. Egil started to head out when he noticed that his client seemed lost and disoriented by it all. "Do you have car fare home?"

"No," Schmidts said. "I didn't have any money on me when they came and arrested me. Not a cent."

"Which way do you live?"

The old man gave an address on Fair Oaks Street. It wasn't far out of his way. Neither one of them lived in the best part of town.

"I can give you a lift," Egil said.

"That's kind of you, Mr. Njalsson," Schmidts said. The mister was ironic. The arrest report hadn't given an age, just "somewhere around seventy." As far as Egil could tell that might have been off by a decade or two.

The address turned out to be a sort of second hand junk store. The operative word was junk. If the pieces in the dirty window were the best of the lot then Egil could see how Schmidts qualified as indigent.

"Thanks for the ride. I've a beer inside if you'd like."

Njalsson looked at his watch. It wasn't too early to start drinking, at least just a beer. The work at the office would wait. He had to talk to Schmidts anyway to prepare a case. Besides, the old man seemed to want to pay him back for the ride.

If anything, the shop was worse on the inside than it looked from the front. Odd bits of bric-a-brac were strewn around everywhere; most of it looking like it hadn't been moved or even dusted in twenty years. Broken down pieces of furniture were covered with moldering sheets.

The old man led him to the back and up some stairs to an apartment above the shop. The kitchen was cleaner, though still hardly spotless. Of course, Egil's own small apartment wasn't the neatest of place, either.

The refrigerator looked as old as Schmidt's, but the beer was cold. Schmidt's took out two and motioned him to a chair at the kitchen table.

"So what happens now, Mr. Njalsson?"

"The trial will be held on the date on the summons. The district attorney will call his witnesses and make his case. Then I'll make my case. The judge will then decide."

"No jury?" Schmidt's asked disappointedly.

"Not unless we've got a very strong case to present. This is a small matter. It's better left to a judge. A jury would be considered a waste of time, I'm afraid, and would probably result in a higher fine. Maybe even jail."

"So you think I'm guilty?"

"I don't think you have much of a case."

"That's different?"

"To a lawyer it is."

Schmidts snorted in disgust.

"I don't want to disillusion you, Mr. Schmidts, but you've got to face the facts. Do you have a license to practice Magic?"

"No."

"Did you tell the fortune of one Mrs. Einar Johnson?"

"Yes, and an ungrateful woman she is, too. Just because I told her the truth about that shifty salesman she thinks is going to marry her. He's just after her late husband's money."

Egil raised an eyebrow.

"It's the truth. I've been reading the cards longer than you've been alive, Mr. Njalsson, and I know what I'm doing. That salesman is the one that got her to swear out a complaint against me."

"It doesn't matter whether what you said was the truth or not. What matters is that you were practicing the Art without a license. Magic is a potentially dangerous business. It's not something that untrained people should be dealing with. That's what the law is about."

"What would you know about the Art, Mr. Lawyer?" Schmidts asked sharply.

"I know more than most, Mr. Schmidts. I studied applied metaphysics at the California Institute of Thaumaturgy for four years before going into the law. I've got a Bachelor's of Science degree. I've also got my practitioner's license from both the state of California and Wisconsin. I may not be the greatest practitioner of the Art, but I am competent enough to know what I am and am not capable of."

"So maybe you did study at a fancy school out west. Those scientists don't know everything. They think that they've discovered magic, but magic goes back. Way back. Back before Helmholtz and Gauss. Before the Egyptians and Babylonians. Magic is old, Mr. Njalsson, and the doctors and professors haven't learned half of it."

"And you have?" Egil asked sarcastically. He was getting annoyed at the old man's pretensions of knowledge. He was surprised, though, that Schmidts knew that the two physicists Helmholtz and Gauss had been instrumental in proving the scientific basis for magic.

"No. I'm no fool. I've been studying the Art all my life. I know what I know and I have a good idea of what I don't. What I do know is more than a youngster like you learns in four years at college, even if it is a fancy one."

"Look, Mr. Schmidts," Egil said. "This isn't working out. Maybe you should get yourself a different lawyer."

The old man looked at him in surprise, then shook his head. "No. I guess you were just telling me the way it is. I may not like it, but I can't fault you for telling the truth."

"Okay. Is there anything I can use in your defense?"

"Guess not."

"Well, where did you learn to tell fortunes, to read the cards?" Egil asked.

"From an old Romany woman," the old man answered.

"Where? Here in the city?"

"No, it was a long time ago. Bohemia, I think it was."

"Bohemia? You mean Czechoslovakia."

"Yes, that's what they call it now I think. Prague. I was a student there."

"A student? At a university? I thought you didn't believe in learning."

"I was younger then. I thought there were things I might learn. I was wrong."

"Did you get a degree, though? That might carry some weight, especially a foreign one."

"Wait a moment. I think I have one someplace. Let me go look." Schmidts went down to his shop. From below Egil could hear noises as if boxes were being moved around. He didn't quite know what to make of the old man's gypsy tale. Bohemia had become part of Czechoslovakia after the First World War in the breakup

of the Austrian Empire. It hadn't been a separate
country since the Hapsburgs.

There were footsteps on the stairway and Schmidts
showed up with a small picture frame carrying a piece of
parchment. It was certainly a degree, but not from the
University of Prague. The writing had faded with age
and Egil had never learned French, but it appeared to be
a doctorate granted by the Sorbonne. It was also made
out to one Jacques Krieger.

"This isn't your name."

"It was the name I was using then."

"Can you prove that?"

"Not that I can see."

"Oh well. Maybe we can use it. If you can find
anymore old papers like this save them for me. We might
have some defense if we can prove you had an education,
particularly if it was before the current examination
system went into effect."

"I'll do that, Mr. Njalsson."

"Well I've got to get going now. Can I take this with
me?" the lawyer asked, holding up the sheepskin.

"Yes, if it will help."

Egil let himself out through the shop. He dumped the
diploma on the car seat next to him and started the car.
While the engine was warming up he glanced down at it.
The date was written in Roman numerals. It took him a
moment to figure out the year. It was 1847. Either the
old man was lying to him or he might find himself
defending him in a commitment hearing.

Also From Resurrected Press

Science Fiction Authors Resurrected

Fyfe Resurrected - The Stories of H. B. Fyfe

Stories from the Golden Age of Science Fiction by the author of *D-99*. dealing with the interaction of humans and aliens on far off worlds in ways that were as creative as they were imaginative.

Bone Resurrected - The Stories of J. F. Bone

More stories from the Golden Age of Science Fiction. Includes "The Issahar Artifact," "Assassin," "To Choke an Ocean" and more.

Nourse Resurrected - The Stories of Alan E. Nourse

Stories from the Golden Age of Science Fiction. Includes "Contamination Crew." "Coffin Cure," "The Link," and more.

Dick Resurrected - The Early Stories of Philip K. Dick

Early stories from the author of the novels that inspired "Blade Runner," "Total Recall," and through a scanner darkly. Science Fiction Authors Resurrected

OTHER CLASSIC SCIENCE FICTION NOVELS BEING RESURRECTED SOON

TALENTS, INCORPORATED - BY MURRAY LEINSTER
When a Mekinese fleet conquers his home planet, Captain Bors turns to Talents, Incorporated for help using their collection of individuals with unusual abilities to defeat the enemy and save the galaxy.

THE PIRATES OF ERSATZ - BY MURRAY LEINSTER
Bran Hodden just wanted to be an electronic engineer and marry a delightful girl. But when he's framed by the powers on Walden he's forced to turn back to his family's trade, piracy. Also published as The Pirates of Zan.

EMPIRE - BY CLIFFORD SIMAK
Spencer Chambers and Interplanetary Power owned the Solar System because they controlled the source of power. It fell to Russell Page and Harry Wilson to challenge that control if they had to cross the universe to do it.

NIGHT OF THE LONG KNIVES - THE CREATURE FROM THE CLEVELAND DEPTHS - BY FRITZ LEIBER
Two classic novellas set in the not too distant future from a classic master of science fiction.

ARMAGEDDON - 2419 A.D. - THE AIR LORDS OF HAN - BY PHILLIP FRANCIS NOWLAN
The two novels that introduced the world to that intrepid hero of the 25th Century, Buck Rogers. Buck Rogers must save the world from the clutches of the insidious Han.

OTHER CLASSIC RESURRECTED SCIENCE FICTION EDITED BY GREG FOWLKES

RESURRECTED MARTIANS
Classic Stories about Mars and Martians from the Golden Age of Science Fiction

RESURRECTED ALIENS
Classic Stories of Aliens and Alien Encounters from the Golden Age of Science Fiction

RESURRECTED FLYING SAUCERS
Classic Stories of Flying Saucers and Alien Invasions from the Golden Age of Science Fiction

RESURRECTED ROBOTS
Classic Stories of Robots, Cyborgs and Androids from the Golden Age of Science Fiction

RESURRECTED SPACE SHIPS -
Classic Stories of Space Ships from the Golden Age of Science Fiction

RESURRECTED TIME TRAVEL
Classic Stories of Time Travel from the Golden Age of Science Fiction

RESURRECTED DIMENSIONS
Classic Stories of other Dimensions from the Golden Age of Science Fiction

RESURRECTED FUTURES
Classic Stories of the Far Future from the Golden Age of Science Fiction

RESURRECTED MAD SCIENTISTS
Classic Stories of Mad Scientists and their Creations from the Golden Age of Science Fiction

RESURRECTED MONSTERS
Classic Stories of Monsters and Mayhem from the Golden Age of Science Fiction

The Fictional Detective
by Greg Fowlkes

Who killed Ezekial O. Handler?

A beautiful dame, a hard-boiled private eye – and a
dead body.

It started like any other case. When a famous writer
dies in a mysterious car crash, private detective
Frank Slade is called in to find answers, but all he
finds is more questions.   Who killed Ezekial
Handler? Who is Janet Nielsen and why is she so
interested in finding out? Who is leaving the neatly
typed clues? And as Slade tries to find answers to
these questions he starts to wonder if the ultimate
answer will threaten his very existence.

Read about it in
The Fictional Detective

Visit www.thefictionaldetective.com

About Resurrected Press

A division of Intrepid Ink, LLC, Resurrected Press is dedicated to bringing high quality, vintage books back into publication. See our entire catalogue and find out more at www.ResurrectedPress.com.

About Intrepid Ink, LLC

Intrepid Ink, LLC provides full publishing services to authors of fiction and non-fiction books, eBooks and websites. From editing to formatting, from publishing to marketing, Intrepid Ink gets your creative works into the hands of the people who want to read them. Find out more at www.IntrepidInk.com.

Made in the USA
Lexington, KY
29 June 2011